who designed the cover for this book and is featured in it.

- John Telford 12/22/'16

THE Poet-Emperor of EARTH

- AN IN-DEPTH DIALOGUE WITH THE DEITY

by

DR. JOHN TELFORD

First Edition

PAGE PUBLISHING, INC.
New York, NY

First originally published by Page Publishing, Inc. 2016

ISBN 978-1-68289-300-5 (Paperback)
ISBN 978-1-68289-304-3 (Digital)

Cover by Donald Frederickson

Printed in the United States of America

Introduction

Prof. Josh Bassett, Director of the Institute for
Social Progress, Wayne County, Michigan

Dr. John Telford is a legendary educator, civil-rights activist, critical race-scholar, accomplished poet, and intrepid social-justice advocate. In his long-ago youth, he was also an audacious world-class athlete known for outrunning Olympic sprinters against whom the "expert" odds-makers had often allotted him little chance. In his allegorical dialogue between earthling and Deity where—as the author himself might say "Let the consequences be damned!"—this famous Michiganian (or *infamous* Michiganian, depending on one's political perspective) takes us through a wild, Dante-esque, only *semi*-fictionalized narrative, drawing upon his eighty years of explosive earthly experience to speak proverbial truth-to-power with no less a Luminary than God 'Himself/Herself/Itself.'

Such forthrightness (or *colloquially*, such "no bullshit allowed") has long been called a privilege of old age—a cited benefit from having paid one's dues and having resolved one's sense of identity vis-à-vis social convention—and having thus been empowered to address bluntly and in depth the ultimate issues that impact humanity. This is the customary course of progress of such events, with *advanced age* offering in some quarters a near-impenetrable social shield. However, unlike with most of us, this has been the 'customary course of progress' in Dr. John Telford's life practically *since the moment he was born,* without benefit of or desire for any sort of 'social shield' *whatever.* Dr. Telford's preternatural fire—his rebelliously democratic compulsion to divert a corporate-dominated world onto a fairer and more humane path in the midst of battling his own inner demons—is writ large across the pages of this book (Telford's fifth within the past five years).

Despite his lyrical and often tragi-comic tone in this allegory in which his own oftentimes tortured persona is only very *thinly* disguised in the character of the old activist-poet protagonist 'John-Paul Jones the Third,' Telford characteristically dares once again to bare his soul in the cause of universal peace-with-justice. As he did in his 2010 autobiography, *A Life on the RUN – Seeking and Safeguarding Social Justice* and in some of his other books and newspaper columns and in his radio and television shows, he has confronted readers of *The* Poet-*Emperor of EARTH* with fundamental questions regarding education, politics, social relations, and the future of democratic government—not only in Detroit and Michigan and all across America—but also throughout the entire planet.

That the activist columnist/poet Telford should choose for this latest book a literary form that follows that of Aristophanes, Dante, Swift, and (contemporarily) Bruce Jay Friedman shouldn't surprise anyone who knows him, has read him, or has worked with him over the last six decades and is familiar with his often earthy humor and his uncompromising indomitableness. From his various insightful analyses of issues of race and class in education and politics to his impassioned call for grassroots action in furthering the fight against the growing hegemonic power of plutocratic entities that busily and frighteningly work to undermine the bedrock principles of the democratic state, he deftly commandeers the fictionalized and anthropomorphized literary form he uses in this allegorical novelette to render viscerally scathing sociopolitical critiques and insightful counsel. Humankind's desperate need to resist this dehumanizing hegemonic power is the overweening message of the book. It is an urgent message that no reader should lose sight of in the midst of this allegory's biting satire—or rather, as the *point* of its biting satire.

My own introduction to John Telford actually followed similar conditions as described above. I was doing research in 2002 on racial segregation in Detroit and its neighboring suburbs. Leading urban-studies scholars like john a. powell (uses no caps), Thomas Sugrue, the late Grace Lee Boggs, Reynolds Farley, Maria Krysan, Douglass Massey, the late Manning Marable, Cornel West, Henry Louis Gates, and noted others have observed that the metropolitan Detroit region has been and remains one of the most crucial locales for understanding racial dynamics in the United States—particularly as our nation enters its historic transformation to a majority multiracial society for the first time in its history. (Several of them incidentally served with Telford on the advisory board of the Institute for Social Progress.)

Like many academics before (and likely after) me, I pored over the abundance of critical work done on the city—the numerous books, hundreds of articles, and countless studies—when suddenly I came across a short but incisive 1999 article in the *Detroit Free Press* titled, 'Race problems stand in the way of true growth,' written by Telford and john a. powell, the former national legal director of the ACLU who later headed up institutes for the study of race and ethnicity at the University of Minnesota and the Ohio State University and now directs one at the University of California-Berkeley. What struck me most about Telford's and powell's approximately 750-word piece was its measured tone, critical scope, and unflinching analysis of how racial segregation operates in Detroit (and in residential areas across the nation) and continues to produce substantial inequalities for primarily African-American and Latino populations.

Given this written introduction to Dr. Telford's work, I expected that when I actually finally met him, I would encounter a similarly measured, patiently thoughtful, somewhat dry and sedentary academician who was professionally devoted to urban education and scholarship. What I found instead is a vibrant, foaming, and absolutely fearless *radical*—a man of *words* and *letters*, certainly, but equally so of *direct and audacious action*—an old academic renegade and catalytic teacher/poet who has always dared to live on ultimate terms that few of us will attempt; namely, to have repeatedly put his livelihood and occasionally even his very *life on the line* in his career-long crusade against injustice.

To read and digest *The* Poet-*Emperor of EARTH – An In-Depth Dialogue with The DEITY* is to become far more than merely amused, edified and enlivened—it is to become at once enlightened, emboldened, and *outraged.* If you read all of this landmark book to the very end, you will also experience a renewed spirit of hope. *The* Poet-*Emperor of EARTH* is a fitting and poetically eloquent addition to poet/author Telford's hefty literary arsenal of weaponry against the forces of evil, for the far greater good of us all. Be aware, too, that once you begin to read this fast-moving book, you won't want (or be able) to put it down until you *have* read it all the way through to the end—and *no peeking at* the *end* until you have read it *all*!

Introductory Poetical/ Biblical/ Philosophical Questions & Quotations

"Have you comprehended the expanse of the Earth? Where is the way to the dwelling of light, *and where is the place of* darkness…*?" - the Biblical Book of* Job

"Did God create us, *or did* <u>*we*</u> *create* <u>God</u>*?" - the intensely* <u>*non*</u>*-Biblical* <u>Books</u> *of* Telford (see www.AlifeontheRUN.com and Amazon Books)

"I *once* thought that like *drunkenness,* blind belief in the existence of a 'DEITY' is *voluntary insanity.*" – rational (and unrecorded) early remark of the *semi*-fictitious 'John-Paul Jones the Third'—the divinely-anointed '*Poet*-Emperor of EARTH'

"Planet Earth has lost *half its wildlife* in the past four decades." – The *Wall Street Journal,* October, 2014. (*Related quote from your esteemed author*: "Time still remains for us to avoid catastrophic global warming and also avoid a planet-wide poisoning of the ecology— but such avoidances *cannot* happen within the current precepts of capitalism.")

"Violence is a descending spiral, begetting the *very thing* it seeks to destroy." – the Rev. Dr. Martin Luther King, Jr.

"...Listen, *listen* / to the *whole Earth* purging / insanity from its [pan-planetary] soul..." – Detroit's pan-cultural Filipina-African-American activist Aurora Harris, a *Howard Zinn* Prize Poet

"We must look to society's *outsiders* to engender society's most radically revolutionary *innovations.*" - the late, great Detroit revolutionary James 'Jimmy' Boggs, *Pages from a Negro Worker's Notebook*; and "We must *also* look to our *poets* for the most radically creative and *evolutionary thinking.*" – semi-imaginary quote of the semi-fictitious poet 'John-Paul Jones III'

Dedication

This allegorical novella is dedicated to the memory of all the murdered men, women, and children in the Czech village of Ledice, to the memory of the millions of Jews, Gypsies, Poles, and other martyrs of the Nazi holocaust, to the memory of the kidnapped and enslaved Africans in the Western Hemisphere between the sixteenth and nineteenth centuries, to the memory of the victims of lynchings in the United States in the twentieth century, to the contemporary victims of America's rising corporatocracy and growing neo-Jim Crowism, to the children poisoned by the Flint River water, and to all mortal Earthlings who love *true democracy* and will *dare*—and if needs be, *die*—to replant its egalitarian seed in America, as well as in all earthly dictatorships.

The book is also dedicated to those *truly* liberal American activists who indeed are determined to *restore* genuine democracy and then to *preserve* and *defend* it in our now overwhelmingly *Incorporated* States of America in the second decade of the twenty-first century.

Finally, it is devotedly dedicated to the *real* 'Balalaika Jones'—that dark and lovely '*Contessa *Adriena,*' my Lady of the Lake and my own *personal Empress*—an uncompromising *democrat* (with both a *small* and a *capital* 'D').

*Detroit & St. Clair Shorian name: *Adrienne Telford*

A Pregnant Prologue

Early on a Sunday afternoon in April, 2014, an activist octogenarian poet named *John-Paul Jones* the *Third*—the recent (and recently *embattled*) Superintendent of the Detroit Public Schools and before that the embattled Superintendent of the nearby Madison District Public Schools—was driving his shiny black Lincoln from his lakefront getaway in St. Clair Shores to his main home in Detroit's 1950s-vintage River House. He was going there to prepare for a radio show he hosted on WCHB NewsTalk1200 which drew thousands of listeners in the tri-county region. His second-time guest was to be [the incidentally very *real* and very *Democratic*] Mark Schauer, a reformist former U.S. Congressman from Battle Creek who was running for Governor [*unsucccessfully*, as it unfortunately was to turn out on November 4, 2014]. Schauer's populist political platform was one that John-Paul Jones the Third fervently shared in every plank of that platform.

Crusty old educator Jones—who incidentally was also an *artist*, a *violinist*, and *particularly* a *poet* with a Delphic bent for societal *prophetizing*—was driving distractedly and rather erratically, because in his mind he was formulating questions that he planned to pose on the air to the gubernatorial candidate at three o'clock that afternoon. For some years, he had also become increasingly concerned about the impending worldwide cataclysm toward which our chronically war-infested planet is plummeting at warp speed at the hands of some misguided leaders. Thus, he was also considering the phrasing of the following apocalyptic poem of ten lines that he intended to recite there as well:

2022: A Prophetic *Plutonium* Poem

We held in '44
Mere *elemental* war.
Before our song is sung,
We'll decompose among
Atomic dust—which, *blown*—
Shall smother seeds unsown.
Before you breathe a *breath*,
Your birthright will be *death*—
Now leaning toward *us*, too,
Just eight short years from *you*.

John-Paul Jones the Third therefore failed to react to the speeding car that ran a stop sign and T-boned him until it was too late for him to avoid the collision. The old talk-show host, who foolhardily hadn't worn his seat belt, was thrown from the car and landed with his balding head hitting the pavement hard. His blood gushed copiously onto the street.

A neighborhood lady who had witnessed the crash grabbed her cell phone out of her purse and called the EMS, which came almost immediately and rushed the now-unconscious educator/poet to St. John Hospital on Seven Mile Road in Detroit. Doctors there operated to relieve pressure on his swelling brain from a deep skull fracture, and they put a steel plate in his head. The accident had also triggered a heart attack which had been waiting to happen, as the old man's main artery to the heart—the one colloquially called the "widowmaker"—had been 100-percent blocked from too many years of fried-chicken consumption. During the same operation, desperate doctors installed a large stent in that artery.

John-Paul's frightened wife Balalaika was informed that he had descended into a deep coma, with odds-on chances that he would never awaken. However, John-Paul had once been a champion quarter-miler, and he still possessed the *heart* of a champion quarter-miler—so two months later, he *did* emerge from the coma seemingly fully recovered. Still languishing in his hospital bed, he began immediately to scribble additional reams of poetry, because beginning early in his long life, penning poem after poem after *poem* had always been his primary passion....

I.

The eighty-year-old Detroit human-rights activist/educator/*poet* with the proud name John-Paul Jones the Third emerged from the brain injury-induced coma with his faculties evidently intact, and his newest poems reflected that lucidity. They also reflected his evolutionary/revolutionary *social activism.*

Accordingly, the first verse he wrote when he awakened in the hospital went like this:

<u>These Un-United States:</u>
<u>The Pachyderm Party of "No"</u>

There's frustration in our nation:
Bureaucracies breed disunity
With plutocratic impunity.

And then he wrote:

<u>To Re-Americanize America</u>

For the sake and salvation
Of our new generation,
Damn its degradation;
Laud its liberation.

The salient solution?—
Revive the *Revolution*

Now!

After that, he wrote:

Comes the *Revolution*

It is unfortunately true
That by Two Thousand Twenty-Two
Those "*one*-percenter" corporate cats
And money-grubbing plutocrats
Who make a fateful mockery
Of our once-great democracy
Shall have had a decade's warning
That the *Revolution's* forming.
All of us should be dissenters—
Black and *white* and *gray* and *gay*.
There can be no weak *relenters*:
Everyone must join the fray!

And then, when he arrived home from the hospital on the 3rd day of July in the Year of our Lord 2014—which coincidentally happened to be his late and sainted mother's 107th birthday—he wrote:

In Dead of Night

Erase the 'N' from *crowNs*, bejeweled
And worn by corporate emperors:
You then get pupil-plucking *crow_s*
Evolved of sable-feathered snakes
That flew through prehistoric nights.

Therefore beware, O mogul Trump
And your own reptilian ilk:

It's but one mere misstep down
From contemporary night
To Revolutionary *nightmare*—
And the black and crow-plucked blindness
Of the *dead.*

And finally, for good measure—believing that the socially insensate bankers and politicians and ravenous corporate sharks may have finally been emotionally moved *too late* (if at all) to consult the gold timepieces in the watch-fobs in the vests of their thousand-dollar, three-piece sharkskin suits, he wrote:

<u>The *Thirteenth* Hour</u>

Xenophobic, ethnocentric, racist, classist kinds
Of misanthropically myopic, microscopic minds
Mask beneath intolerance a frightful face of fear
That's globally infectious—the *Holocaust* is here.

Then, on the Fourth of July in the Year of our Lord 2014, it resultantly came to pass that a Divine and miraculous Entity That/Who might best be called "**GOD THE GREAT ETERNAL PRESENCE**"—Who/Which had been thoughtfully monitoring the prophet poet John-Paul Jones the Third's most recent righteously incendiary and prophetic poeticizing—thereby incredibly chose from *on high* to communicate *directly* to the now apparently fully recovered old poet. Over the past several centuries, God the Great Eternal Presence had become a connoisseur of some of the better earthly poetry and indeed a rather *rabid Fan* of some of the better Earthling poets. He/She/It had particularly favored Homer, Horace, Virgil, Milton, Shakespeare (the Sonnets), Robert Burns, William Wordsworth, W. B. Yeats, Henry Wadsworth Longfellow, Walt Whitman, Federico Garcia Lorca, Dylan Thomas, T. S. Eliot, Dudley Randall, Vachel Lindsay, A. E. Housman, LeRoi Jones (AKA Amiri Baraka), Emily Dickenson, Langston Hughes, M. L. Liebler, Aurora Harris, Carolyn

Forché, and sometimes Robert Frost and Nikki Giovanni (but *never* Ezra Pound).

He/She/It was also of the firm opinion that no human being could make a fine, upright *statesman* unless that human being were also a fine, upright *poet* with a decidedly innovative and occasionally *insurrectionary* temperament.

The Divine Presence therefore revealed to the so-recently comatose but now awakened and alert poet John-Paul that because this recent invalid's revolutionist poetry was *proof-positive* that he shared His/Her/Its pessimistically troubled views concerning current *faux*-democratic human leadership and humankind's precariously uncertain fate, He—or *It*—had now decided to anoint this wise old poet to become the impending and benign *Emperor* of this beautiful blue-green globe called *Earth*, that third planetary pebble out from one particular blazingly golden sun-speck of star in the vast and untold universe that He/It had so divinely fashioned.

However, John-Paul the Poet just happened to be extremely *non*-superstitious—and indeed, if not an *almost*-atheist, at least a confirmed *agnostic*. Therefore, rather than gathering that he had miraculously received a *direct message from God*, he presumed that he was simply "hearing" nebulous noises that consisted of deceptively meaningful but actually metallic, meaningless sounds accidentally emanating from some manner of electro-magnetic wave via the steel plate that surgeons had so recently embedded in his head. He alternatively assumed that these sounds might have manifested themselves either as an after-effect of his still relatively recent auto accident, or even perhaps—*God forbid*—as a result of encroaching *senility.* He also speculated that he could be "hearing" them simply because he had consumed *too much scotch* the previous evening when he'd been hosting a gathering of friends and relatives in his spacious lakefront yard on Lake St. Clair in the city of St. Clair Shores in the Michigan county of Macomb, U.S.A.

Although he was a bit woozy from a slight hangover, it also occurred to him that perhaps he might have "heard" the sounds as a result of his having eaten *three possibly tainted eggs* for breakfast that morning that his wife Balalaika had forgetfully left for over a month in the kitchen refrigerator.

Thus, John-Paul not only chose to ignore this Message from the Entity that had revealed Itself to him as "GOD THE GREAT ETERNAL PRESENCE," but he also tried very nervously and very *hard* to convince himself that he had never even *heard* this so-called *Eternal Presence's* mysterious Message. However, this earnest endeavor on his part proved to be fruitless, because the *Presence* doggedly continued to din and dun Its tinny but nonetheless genuinely divine and holy Message deep into the old man's brain via the metal plate in his head.

On the day after his having first heard this divine Message—which in actuality he *had* indeed truly heard and heard all too *clearly*—he was sitting in his living room in what could best be described as an escalating state of distressed distraction from the piercing, persistent Voice. It was then that he found himself finally realizing that something far beyond the ordinary could really be happening to him, and he knew he was going to have to try to confront it.

"Okay, Mr. *Presence*, or *Whoever* or *Whatever* you are," he announced loudly and challengingly to the Presence, "if You're really and truly God the Great Divine and Eternal Presence, give me some kind of divine sign that You're what You *say* You are."

At this point, his wife Balalaika—a dark-haired beauty of Russian Jewish ancestry who had been daintily arranging dishes in the kitchen dishwasher—heard his words and called to him, "John-Paul, who on *earth* are you talking to?"

"I think that I may actually be *communicating* with God the Great Eternal Presence! Please don't interrupt my train of thought, Balalaika."

"Oh, I'm sorry—I didn't know you were praying—I never knew you to be much for *prayer*. What are you so *uncharacteristically* praying about? Is everything all right?"

"Honey, you're going to think this is really weird, but I believe that this so-called 'Eternal Presence' here might have been telling me that It has appointed me to be the *Emperor of Earth*!"

"*Oy vey*, JP—an 'Eternal Presence?' 'Emperor of the *Earth*?' What kind of nonsense is *that*? Is this another one of your practical jokes? If it is, it's not a *bit* funny. Are you pulling my leg, or what? Or did you maybe get into the liquor cabinet again? If you did, I guess I'm finally going to have to lock the damned thing up! That whiskey is going to make you *fat*."

John-Paul Jones the Third had been born and raised in a frame house in one of the few racially integrated lower-class neighborhoods in Detroit. He was a first-generation Scots-American whose hard-drinking father, John-Paul Jones the Younger and hard-drinking grandfather John-Paul Jones had been Scotland-born coal miners, prizefighters, and factory workers who could trace their ancestry directly to the American naval captain John Paul Jones, that great nautical neutralizer of English King George III's vaunted Royal Navy some two hundred years earlier. Most of John-Paul Jones the Third's father's Highland family had been alcoholics, but while he himself did enjoy a nip or two on a daily basis, he didn't regard himself as an alcoholic, so he resented his wife's threat to lock up the liquor.

"Balalaika," said he, "I haven't had a single *drop* of alcohol today. I'm telling you I really *have* been hearing this Message from some ethereal 'Presence'—and it's not out there in the stratosphere somewhere, either. It's actually very *close by*—like almost in the same *room* with me. I've been hearing Its *Message* in my head again and again and *again*—and I'm not drunk and I'm not crazy. I'm trying now to *channel* It again this very minute and get It to show me some kind of physical sign that It *is* what It *says* It is. If you want to be *around* me right now, you're going to have to keep quiet so I can concentrate on this."

At that precise moment, God the Great Eternal Presence resonantly intoned the following words through the conducting metal plate in John-Paul's head, deep into John-Paul's brain:

John-Paul, my son—what do you wish to be done *in order for you to believe in Me and become thus convinced?*

"I'll tell you what I wish to be done," John-Paul answered It excitedly and challengingly. "If You're really *God*, I'm sure You can pilot an unmanned watercraft with no one visibly at the wheel, right?"

He pointed to his sleek 21-foot Sea Ray sitting on a hoist by a cement sea wall at the edge of the huge lake. "See that speedboat? I want you to remove its canvas cover and lower it to the water, start its engine, and take it sixty yards out onto the lake and drive it in a wide circle within clear sight of the shore at a speed of precisely *50mph* and then bring it back, turn off the engine, and put it on the hoist again and raise it—and then put its cover back on securely."

As soon as that last word had been uttered, God the Great Eternal Presence made it all happen, with the sleek speedboat's inboard/outboard 350 hp motor roaring and spitting up a good-sized "rooster tail" in its wake.

"Omigod, Bala!" John-Paul shouted in an unwitting pun, ambling on his cane fast and excitedly into the kitchen. "You heard the challenge I gave to the Godly Presence—and then did you *see that*? Wow! Did you *see that*?"

In a state of near stupefaction, he understood now that the Divine Eternal Presence was indeed what It had *claimed* to be, and he also realized immediately that Balalaika had indeed *heard* his challenge to It and had *witnessed* this *incredibility*...

...and that sometime during the course of the Divine Eternal Presence's miraculous nautical demonstration, she had fallen face-down on the floor in a frightened, flat-out-prostrate faint.

II.

On the sixth of July, 2014, precisely at noon in the United States' Eastern Standard Time Zone of Planet Earth's Western Hemisphere, God the Great Eternal Presence followed up Its earlier interactions with John-Paul Jones the Third by intoning unto him,

John-Paul Jones the Third, I want you to tell your wife that you are going to take a nap *and you don't* want *to be* disturbed!

Since the eighty-year-old John-Paul *had* in fact been *napping precisely at that time*, the Presence's booming intonement had *awakened* him, so he said, "I don't *need* to tell her that, Your Godliness. She already *knows* I'm napping—or rather, now, that I *was* napping!"

All right—then tell her that this Entity Which (or Whom) you address as 'My Godliness' is going to put you in a trancelike state for a couple of Earth-hours, and you're not to be disturbed unless the house catches on fire or the Iranians or North Koreans or perhaps Isis *hit your tightly tidy little city of St. Clair Shores with a thermonuclear bomb.*

"*What*?! Is my *house* going to catch on fire or a *bomb* land on us? Is this going to be *dangerous*?"

No, of course *not. I just don't want her to* awaken *you. Do you see the beautiful white expanse of cumulous clouds reaching to a sweeping width of several miles and rising to a height of nearly a thousand feet over*

your lake? I'm going to be sitting somewhere inside it near its peak in that vault of blue flame which you Earthlings call your "sky." I'll be in the form of a muscular old man with a white beard, and I'll have your favorite 'rusty nail' on ice [scotch and Drambuie] *waiting for you when I transport your living spirit up there so we can chat.*

God the Great Eternal Presence was as good as Its word: John-Paul Jones the Third presently found himself sitting in what appeared to be an armchair of what appeared to be Corinthian leather in what appeared to be a brightly lit, magnificently furnished room in the sky. The Divine Eternal Presence sat in what appeared to be a similar chair facing him. Its/His Appearance to John-Paul was that of an identical facsimile of Michelangelo's soaring frescoed Sistine Chapel depiction of God the Father and Creator of Mankind extending a Fatherly fingertip to give life to Adam.

So, my prophetically <u>poeticizing</u> *friend—does your 'rusty nail' have a suitable and correct amount of Drambuie?*, the Eternal Presence inquired solicitously of John-Paul the Poet.

"God, *yes*—er, I mean, *yes*, God, thank You. But how can I be up here actually drinking these 'rusty nails' with Your Divinity when I'm really down by the lake napping on a sofa in my living room? I guess it's possible because at this moment I'm my out-of-body transported *spirit*, right?"

John-Paul, you need to be aware that being of mortal humankind and of My making, you are and will remain a spirit <u>eternally</u>, *whether you be physically alive or* post-*physically* dead. *However, just because your current presence with Me is incorporeal at this point in cosmic time, while your* conscious self *is temporarily in an* <u>entirely</u> spiritual *form, that doesn't mean that you are unable to experience the* sensation *of* drinking *a* 'rusty nail!' *I have now given you that ability. Know ye that I can generate and empower* <u>anything</u>, *because I am* <u>God</u>, *the* Great *Spirit in the Sky.*

The Presence paused; Its dark eyes in Its borrowed Michelangelic countenance burned like two bits of coal as they focused intently on John-Paul from beneath bushy white eyebrows.

I note that you polished off that 'rusty nail' pretty fast, the Presence observed. *Here—let me pour you another, and maybe one* more *as well—but no* <u>more</u> *after that, because Up Here it has the same effect on your* <u>spiritual</u> *brain as it would down there on your* physical *one: You and I need to get down to some* <u>serious</u> <u>business</u> *while I'm still keeping this majestically mammoth cloud intact.*

"Okay, Your Godliness—we can talk about that 'Emperor of Earth' stuff You've been mentioning if You like, even though since You are *all-knowing*, You must *know* that I'm not much for *empires* of *any* kind."

Becoming a bit surprised at his own growing impertinence in the fearsome Face of God Incarnate, John-Paul downed another 'rusty nail' and added, "*However*, with Your Godship's permission, first I want to tell You a joke in which You play a *key* part!"

All right, John-Paul, the Presence said somewhat snappishly, fingering Its simulated long white beard with plainly evident impatience. *Go ahead and tell it—but make it a* <u>quick</u> *one.*

John-Paul gave his own white beard a little tug, took the elastic band out of his long pony tail, and shook his graying brown hair loose. He finished his third drink and smacked his lips. Then he leaned back in his chair and put his feet up on a curiously solid yet indistinctly *phantom* footstool.

"Well," he began in a voice that had started to slur slightly, "it seems that once upon a time, You told an extraordinarily righteous old man that as a reward for his *righteousness*, You wanted to grant him his fondest wish. The old man was a motorcyclist who still was wont to traverse the country on his Harley, so he asked You to build him a bridge from California to Hawaii in order for him to be able to ride there across the vast ocean on his cycle and feel the sea breeze. You responded, 'I can do that, of course, because I'm *God*—but I would have to install girders down deep into the ocean floor in order to grant that wish. Besides, I was hoping that you'd wish for something more *socially conscious.*'

"The old man replied to You, 'Well, God, then give me the power to understand all of my *wife's* ever-changing moods and show me a way to empathize with her regarding '*today's* crisis.'

"You pondered for only a brief moment and then You asked the old man, 'Do you want the highway to be *one* lane or *two*?'"

At that, the Great Eternal Presence chuckled rumblingly and divinely and said, *Yes, I remember that joke. I first encountered it in a book entitled* What OLD MEN Know *that was written by a renegade educator named* Telford, *one of your scruffier fellow Michiganians. The joke is quite chauvinistic, but its author really* isn't*—and I don't think that* you *really are either, because I have noted that you are almost uncannily* like *him—and indeed, you write poetry that is even* more *uncannily similar to* his*—except* yours *is* better. *You both even used to* color your beards *in a pathetic and clearly* futile *effort to try to look young.*

"Your Godliness, I didn't dye my beard to 'try to look young'—I did it because it wasn't very full and you could hardly *see* it unless I colored the *white* in it. I have always hated to *shave*, and I didn't care to waste time or money going to the barber. It cut into my *poem*-writing time. Also, if Your Godship won't be offended by my saying so, You remind *me* of something, too: You bring to my mind Michelangelo's fresco depicting You that I saw on a high ceiling in the Vatican in Rome many years ago when I was a sprinter on the United States track team, and Pope Pius XII—then Your 'Emissary on Earth'—personally placed his Papal Medal in my hand."

Yes—Michelangelo was one of my gifted children whom I Divinely *inspired, although Pope Pius XII was far less so: That particular Pope had become a little too cozy with the Nazis and with Italy's fascist government during the Second World War. However, it needs to be recognized that Pope Pius was in a difficult and vulnerable situation with the formidable military juggernaut of the barbaric Austria-born anti-Christ who wore the square little black mustache and that swastika armband.*

Of all the graphic representations of Me generated by humans over the millennia, Michelangelo's in the Vatican happens to be the one I usually favor, so I have assumed that Apparition at this time—the first time that I have ever appeared to a human in a manifest facial image, rather than in a burning bush or a lightning bolt or a rumble of thunder in the sky, so you should feel immensely proud *of yourself.*

Now let Me get to my reason for contacting you:

After giving the world of humankind myriad chances throughout at least *the past six thousand Earth years, I your God and your Creator have come to the unhappy conclusion that you gremlinesque human beings are sadly* incapable *of governing yourselves* democratically *and therefore must be governed by a* benign *king or a* just *emperor. After long and careful reflection and also after ruminating upon your several specifically and righteously* insurrectionist *verses, I have chosen* you *to be that Earthly sovereign. Two particularly* prophetic *poems you wrote several years ago solidified my choice of you. One of them which you wrote way back in the 1950s was entitled 'The Riddle.' It featured a question-and-answer dialogue between a Socratically influenced, anthropomorphized* planet Earth *and a* deux-ex-machina-*style* Oracle *Which in some ways* could conceivably *have been* I, *your Deity.*

Here is how your poem went:

Now 'know_thyself,' said Socrates,
So tell me: *Who* am *I*?

You're mother to theocracies,
Autocracies, bureaucracies,
And blinding-bright technocracies
That tame the solar sky.

Why,
I grant some ideocracies
Were buried by bureaucracies,
But 'Know thyself,' said Socrates,
So tell me what I *do*.

You harbor old hypocrisies
And arid aristocracies.
You nurture corporatocracies
That toll the end *of you!*

What then of my *democracies*?
The highly moral minds among
My wisest children far outrun
The rank morass of vacuous *class*.
Next week I'll likely span
My seed beyond the stars.
Today I simply plan
To speed some sons to Mars.
(I wish they'd quit their quibbling, though,
And come and sit—the Sibling Show
Is being re-run the thousandth time on late TV—
The Backward Gun—and now The *Climb Back to the Tree.*)

Yes, and see—
Suddenly,
The Crime of Cain *begins again*
(As forward runs the reel);
The cries of pain resound in vain.
Too far away to feel,
One errant offspring conjures up

A mighty mushroom tree;
Son Two cuts down the buttercups;
Son Three ignites the sea—
Thus each misguided brother
Annihilates his other.

John-Paul mused in response, "Yes, Your Godship, I wrote that poem way back when I was just a kid in my early twenties, and I still worry today about us humans *annihilating* ourselves. I was always obsessively fascinated with Socrates, and even more with Plato. Back in ancient Greece, four centuries before Your Biblical Son Jesus was even *born*, those two eminent Greek philosophers were widely lauded for their wisdom. One day a young Athenian approached the great Plato with respectful deference and asked, 'Worshipful sir, do you know what I just heard about your student, Aristotle?'

"Plato responded, 'No, I don't, young fellow; but wait just a *minute*—before I let you tell me something about one of my students, I expect you first to pass a little test that I call the Triple Filter Test. The first Filter is *Truth*. Have you *ensured* that what you're about to tell me is *true*?'

"'No, sir,' the student said. 'Actually, I just *heard* about it.'

"'All right, said Plato. 'So you really don't know for sure whether it's *true*. The Second Filter is *Goodness*. Is what you're about to tell me about my good student Aristotle something *good*?'

"'Well, *no*—really, it isn't.'

"'That's *still* all right,' said Plato. 'You *still* may pass the test. The Third Filter is the Filter of *Usefulness*. Is what you want to tell me about Aristotle going to be *useful* to me?'

"'No, most wise and eminent Plato—not *really*.'

"'Then,' the great Plato concluded, 'if what you want to tell me is neither *True* nor *Good* nor even *Useful*, why would you *tell* it to me or to anyone at all?'

The young man was bewildered and ashamed. To him, this was a demonstration of why Plato was such a wise and distinguished philosopher and was held in such lofty esteem, and he went away extremely impressed.

"It also explains why Plato never found out that Aristotle was banging his wife."

John-Paul, that was a terrible *joke—the first one you told me was much better. And Plato didn't even* have *a wife, as I recall. You can thank* Me*—and your Estabrook Elementary School literature teacher Mrs. Hattie Spurck—that you're a far better* poet *than you are a teller of* bad jokes. *Your poem 'The Riddle' was the* first *poem of yours that really* piqued *my* interest *in you. Here is the* second *one, which you wrote ten years later and metaphorically and alliteratively entitled 'Rex Reborn':*

Huger than the heaving ferns,
Looming higher than a hill,
The thunder thing at night returns
To seek and find and pounce and kill.

Jungle fires in the night
Flicker into spreading flame
To cast their blazing, blood-red light
Upn the hunter's hiding game.

Found, the tiny quarry flees:
Teeth like scimitars gleam wet
And drip, descending, pierce and seize—
The killer gulps and rears erect.

Body shining slimy red,
Horrid red the staring eye,
Tyrannosaurus turns its head
To move against the midnight sky.

Might once more in fiery glare
On a *new* primeval heath
A brute stalk forth to crush and tear
And cancel *history* in its teeth??

John-Paul, at the time you wrote 'Rex Reborn,' I Divinely divined that the monstrous reptile which was the subject of that poem was the threat (in metaphor) of U.S.-Soviet mutual mass nuclear annihilation. The USSR has since been partitioned, but that same "brute' whereof you so prophetically *wrote now possesses the potential to raise its brutish head again* here, there, *and* everywhere*—and indeed may have done so in the Ukraine as I speak. Your* extraordinary prescience *as eloquently evidenced in your* poetry*—coupled with your passionate concern for the future health and welfare of your seven billion fellow human beings—is what has made you My* uppermost *and now My* final *choice to assume the mantle of* Emperor of Earth, *and I don't want to hear you tell me any piddling* jokes *about it!*

"O Most Holy Eternal Presence, there will be no more 'piddling' jokes from me, I promise. You have rendered me *speechless* and *humble*—two conditions ordinarily utterly *foreign* to my character. You do great honor unto the planet Earth as well as unto this unworthy Earthling, but why have you chosen *Earth* and its human inhabitants to reform in this manner?? There must be *millions* of other planets with sentient beings on them! Are we Earthlings indeed so *obtuse* and so *errant in our ways* that Your Godliness has singled us out for Your Divine attention?

Yes, your species actually has been *that* errant, *John-Paul. And you're* right *that there are other planets with sentient and indeed highly* intelligent *beings—many of them far* more *so, in fact, than are any of you* Earthlings. *There exist millions of planets with trillions of cognizant creatures of My creation in the Crab and Bear* nebulas alone*—constellations that your fellow human beings have* christened*—if you'll excuse the expression—the 'Crab' and 'Bear' nebulas after an earthly mammal and an earthly crustacean whose outlined star formations in your night sky ancient humans saw them as* resembling. *A very rare and precious* few *of those ultra-intelligent beings of My creation have learned to govern themselves lovingly and peaceably.*

Thus, they do not need the attention from Me that your *quarrelsome, uncaring species needs so desperately. Others out in the untold galaxies in the epochal past have needed to have Me do for them what I am now about to do for you and your grubby kind.*

"Your Godship, please don't believe for a minute that I am ungrateful for Your having tapped me for this divine honor. My gratitude is greater than I am able to express."

John-Paul gazed deep and questioningly into the simulated coal-black eyes of the Great Eternal Presence.

"Still, I have to *ask*—why *me*? Your Godship has spoken disparagingly of *democracy*, and since you are *all-knowing* and are therefore familiar with my more *activist* poetry and my other egalitarian writings, Your Godliness must *know* that I'm a fervid proponent of *democracy*. While being *imperfect* in that *all* forms of government devised by men are *imperfect*, democracy is still by far the best of an *imperfect* lot."

In theory, *you're* right *about* democracy, *John-Paul—but human leaders elected* democratically *in the relatively recent past have too often proved to be venal, corrupt, sometimes even* stupid, *and susceptible to bribes. Too often they were also elitist, nepotistic, cronyist, cruel, ethnocentric, egocentric, racially and religiously* discriminatory, *and* majoritarian *in their approach to* governing, *in their approach to* legislating, *and in their approach to* judging.

And all of this has been singularly *true in your* own *previously democratic country. It hasn't dawned on the corporate moguls down there yet, but when millions of your middle-class countrymen of all races and creeds have become unable to feed their families by legal means, they are damn well going to un-rack their hunting rifles, aim them at targets other than* deer, *and revolt bloodily against their corrupt government. This Second American Revolution is on a current course to occur just eight short years from now, as you so presciently predict in two of your* poems.

I have therefore now finally come to realize that my having granted humankind the privilege of having free will *was a grievous* error, *albeit also by* definition, *a* Divine *one. Far too many of your kind have wreaked unspeakable indecencies and atrocities upon their fellows, rather than practice My Golden Rule.*

I have also therefore finally come to believe that a benign monarchy *or a fair* dictatorship *is the best form of government for ruling what I'm embarrassed to have to admit is your seriously* flawed species *that I have so* imperfectly *created.* Mea culpa, Mea culpa!

"Your Godliness, I do understand that You are all-*seeing*, so I must confess that I *don't* understand why you don't seem to *see* that the concept of a *fair dictatorship* is an *oxymoron*—a contradiction in terms. A dictatorship by its very *definition* can't be *fair*. Dictators are in effect *terrorists* whose deeds are even more *evil* than, say, the militarist killings over the diamond-mining in Sierra Leone or the contemporary kidnappings and ransomings by Somali pirates."

Seeking some more "liquid courage," John-Paul took yet another swallow of his third 'rusty nail,' and blurted, "There are so *many* chillingly dictatorial *examples*—ancient Persia's Xerxes, the Pharaohs of Egypt, Alexander of Macedon, and the Roman Emperors Caligula and Nero, Genghis Khan, Attila the Hun...

Yes, John-Paul—but they all lived a very long time ago.

"Well, more recently there were medieval England's King John, Russsia's Ivan the Terrible, Emperor Henry V of the 'Holy' Roman empire during the Renaissance, Vlad the Transylvanian Impaler, England's Henry VIII, Spain's Philip II, Oliver Cromwell during the so-called 'Protectorate' in mid-seventeenth-century England after the beheading of King Charles I, France's Louis XIV and a century later the Emperor Napoleon, England's George III, Mexico's Porfirio Diaz, Russia's Czar Nicholas II and its current potentate president Vladimir Putin, Germany's Kaiser Wilhelm II and Adolf Hitler, the Soviet Union's Josef Stalin, Italy's Benito Mussolini, Communist China's Mao Tze Tung, Egypt's King Farouk, Iran's Shah Mohammad Reza Pahlavi, Argentine president Juan Peron, Cuban dictator Fulgencio Batista, Tanzania's Idi Amin, Cambodia's Pol Pot, Haitian 'President-for-life' 'Papa Doc' Duvalier, and Sei Seke Mobutu of the former 'Republic' of Zaire. Were those oppressive oligarchs *recent* enough for You?"

John-Paul wiped his brow and searched the Presence's Countenance for some sign that he had got his point across with these more recent and equally chilling examples. Then, since he was addressing *God*, he decided to add some *religious* leaders:

"There was even the warlike seventeenth-century French prime minister Armand Jean du Plessis de Richelieu, the persecutor of the Huguenots—and a Cardinal of the *Church*, if You will!"

He wiped his brow apprehensively and took yet another swallow.

"And then there were those *other* Catholic churchmen—professed disciples of *Yours*, I believe—who burned Jews and other so-called 'heretics' at the stake during the Inquisition!"

Summoning more courage, he added daringly, "And there was that murderous *Pope Alexander VI*—Your *own* 'Emissary on Earth' more than five centuries ago—and his ruthless *offspring* Cesare Borgia!"

He paused to suck in a short breath.

"Also, I could cite the Turks' *massacre* of the Armenians, Europeans' *enslavement* of Africans, and Europeans' committing *genocide* upon indigenous peoples *all across the face of the Earth....* Indeed, I could go on and *on* and *on....*"

My son, most of those men whom you just named behaved brutally, *and they ruled with great* cruelty. *My goal is to* obliterate *slavery and genocide—both of which still occur or threaten to occur on parts of your planet at this very moment.*

You tout your own precious "democratic" nation— but some of your country's presidents *have been* equally guilty *of crimes against humanity. Remember what Andrew Jackson and other presidents did to the Native Americans. Remember what Lyndon Johnson did to the Vietnamese—and to his own fallen soldiers and their grieving families in a war that never should have happened. Years later, his Secretary of State apologized to those grieving families for costing them the lives of their loved ones in that unjust war.*

And I know *that you remember what* George W. Bush *did to the Iraqis and the Afghans—and also to his own fallen servicemen and their heart-broken wives and children—in a war fought over* money *and over* oil, *and rationalized by the* monstrous lie *that he and his Vice President told your countrymen about nonexistent "weapons of mass destruction."*

God stroked Its simulated Michelangelan beard reflectively.

*John-Paul, allow Me to point out that you overlook the fact that I included the word "*benign*" in describing the nature and inclination of* *the monarch who will govern the empire of all humankind that I have finally come to envision for Planet Earth.*

Let me also incidentally add that neither Pope Pius XII nor Pope Alexander VI did I ever *accept as* My *"Emissaries." Don't assume that I am limited to being the God of only* Christians. *I am the God of* all of the species *Homo Sapiens, including Muslims, Buddhists, Jews, animists, polytheists, pagans, pantheists, and* tree-worshippers*! I am even the God of* atheists*—and, indeed, of* agnostics*—including recently* former *ones like* yourself.

Know, too, that I am He Whom the Native Americans worship as the Great Spirit in the Sky. *In that regard, I am going to tell you where men with pale faces like yours went wrong: Many years ago I had a spiritual dialogue with the Lakota Chief Sitting Bull. I told him, "You have observed the white man for many years. You have seen his pistols and rifles and Gatling Gun and his steam engine and his other technological advances. You've seen both his progress, and the sinister damage he's done.'*

'Yes, Great Spirit, that is true,' the chief replied to Me.

I then asked him, "Considering all these events, in your opinion where did the white man go wrong?"

The chief gazed up at Me and answered, "When white man find land, we were living on it and caring *for it but not* owning *it. No taxes, no debt, plenty buffalo, plenty beaver, clean water, women did all the work. Chief free, medicine man free. Braves spend all day hunting and fishing; make love with squaw and plant papooses in them all night."*

Then the old chief leaned back and smiled up at Me and said:

"Only white man DUMB enough *to think he could improve on a system like* that*!"*

John-Paul laughed out loud. "God—er, I mean, Your *Godliness*—that was a *good* one! And there actually was a whole lot of *truth* to it. You'll be glad to know that I've got a plan that resembles Chief Sitting Bull's 'system' in many ways."

I am anxious to hear about your plan, John-Paul, because being familiar with your poetry, I know how you think. It has taken a couple hundred years for the faithless philistines who don't have your humaneness or your hard-earned wisdom to bring Me to the brink of public <u>execution</u> *on Earth—as some misguided "philosophers" who in falsely pronouncing me* <u>dead</u> *have endeavored to do. The* bottom line *is that I* <u>am</u> *and will eternally* <u>remain</u> *the* <u>Living</u> God *and Creator of every* living thing *in the entire universe.*

Having proclaimed all of this, the Eternal Presence rose from Its swiftly dematerializing armchair, and Its white beard and Its long, flowing white raiment began to become one with the blinding whiteness of the mountainous cloud.

Seeing the Divine and Eternal Presence starting to disappear, John-Paul blurted quickly, "*Yes*, Your Godliness, it's *true* that I would be a fair, benign, and egalitarian ruler, but I am old and will not/*could* not rule for long! What if my successor weren't so *benign*?"

John-Paul, there isn't time now for Me to answer that. This gorgeous alabaster cloud that has hosted and housed Us so hospitably this afternoon is disintegrating fast, and I'm not inclined to put it back together, so I am returning briefly to my distant celestial throne and restoring you to your corporeal state. You possibly may physically awaken from your trance with what you English-speaking Earthlings colloquially call a "hangover," and I suggest that you take further rest today due to your advanced Earth-age.

My next conversation with you will commence at precisely six o'clock tomorrow morning in a quiet place down by the cement break-wall of your large lake, at which time a severe summer storm will be approach-

ing. I will divert the storm toward the west throughout our dialogue, during which you will be able to hear Me but not see Me even though I will at that time happen to still be graphically configured as Michelangelo depicted me. I will be hovering unseen behind some clouds that I will keep in the area to shelter your eyes from the glare and your skin from the burning heat of the rising sun, and I will endeavor tomorrow to allay your concerns and begin to describe My Plan for you and your kind.

I would bid you now to go with God, *were it not for the fact that I Myself* am *God, and I am* with *you already.*

III.

At precisely six o'clock the next morning, John-Paul Jones the Third was stretched out comfortably if somewhat still sleepily on one of the all-weather steel-mesh lounge chairs on his cement walkway by the water under an overcast sky when the Eternal Presence announced Itself.

Good morning, John-Paul. I am ready now to respond to the question you put to me yesterday. The answer to your question is this*: You will never* have *a successor as the Emperor of Earth unless you fail to achieve what I* want *you to achieve—and I know how* intolerant *you are of failure of any kind. I intend to keep you and all of your fellow human beings—your subjects who are alive today—in a suspended state of perpetual life in their current physical state. Infants will remain infants; children will remain children; adults young and old will remain as they are forever. Pregnant women will deliver their babies one last time in the new and eternal Empire of Earth and—while they will be able to continue to enjoy copulating with their husbands (and* only *with their husbands, let Me hasten to add), they will never experience pregnancy again.*

When millions of years in the future your sun is about to go dark in the sky, you and your kind will by then have attained the knowledge and skill to have assembled a vast fleet of aircraft-carrier-sized, self-sustaining spacecraft upon which you will venture beyond your solar system and spread your seed even beyond the outer universe into and unto infinity.

However, that's obviously not a consideration for you at this time. There is more infinitely immediate *work to be done on this brightly dawning day of Earthly time-space.*

John-Paul was, in a word, stunned to hear the part about the Eternal Presence's promise to establish a state of *perpetual human life*, nor was he as overjoyed about it as the Presence had expected he would be.

"Your Godliness," he said, "I have but two grandchildren, a ten-year-old grandson and a six-year-old granddaughter. My *daughter*—whose mother, my first wife whom I cheated on repeatedly and egregiously—has misguidedly kept her children from me. I had hoped to perhaps become re-acquainted with them as adults and have *great*-grandchildren that I also could *know* before I died."

You're far too old to have been able to hope for either of those things under previous conditions, My son. Besides, when your daughter becomes aware of your Divinely-anointed role in this New World Order that I envision for the human beings that inhabit your planet, she will undoubtedly recognize the error of her ways and decide that she no longer will deprive her children of their loving grandfather. Also, if I am not mistaken (and I am never mistaken*), was it not one of your own human originators of Western thought—the philosopher* Aristotle*—in following his colleague* Socrates' *lead, who suggested that a* poet *(such as* you*) can minister even to* mortals *who are so mad as to insist that they should be* immortal*? Well, now they* shall *be! And so shall* you *be, like it or* not.

In any case, you must put familial and other personal concerns aside: With the power I am about to grant you comes the awesome responsibility to ensure the wellbeing and creature-comfort of every single one among those approximately seven-plus billion members of your species who live today to whom I will grant this miraculous boon of immortality. *Ensuring their comfort and well-being was a fundamental part of what your vaunted* democracy *was* supposed *to do, but* didn't. *In your nation that is called the "*United *States of America" as it* disunitedly *exists now—and as you have indicated in your poem—the richest* one percent *control* ninety percent *of the wealth, and the poorest ten percent have* nothing. *Some* democracy!

Throughout the globe you call "Earth," *much of the rest of humankind has* little *or* nothing *as well and is agonizingly enmeshed in perpetual warfare and suffering and hopelessness and hunger and thirst and dying.*

All of this will change eternally *for your species with* My Plan, *and today I charge you with beginning to put it in place and make it* happen.

"Your Godliness, once again I must ask: Why *me*? 'Can't You bring back *Moses,* or *Socrates*, or Simon Peter the Fisherman—or else at least Mohandas Ghandi, or Mother Teresa, or Thurgood Marshall, or Queen Elizabeth I, or Eleanor Roosevelt, or Anwar Sadat, or Golda Meir, or Dag Hammarskjold, or Reinhold Niebuhr, or David Ben Gurion, or Robert F. Kennedy, or Martin Luther King, Jr., or someone of their stature?

"Or how about *Nelson Mandela*? The world just recently *lost* him, and he was almost universally lauded—even by South African *whites*. He would command almost limitless respect."

Nelson Mandela*? Are you aware that your American president put him on a list of* terrorists *to watch—and his name wasn't removed until* 2008*?*

"That was President *Reagan*, Your Godship. He took lots of naps, and one of his security officials probably stupidly and erroneously did it in his name. I believe they did a lot of covert things without him even being aware of it, such as the Iran-Contra skullduggery."

No, Reagan did it himself.

"Well, then, Your Godship, that wasn't a very nice thing for President Reagan to do. However, he was an overblown ex-movie star and a turncoat Democrat who went *Republican* and became addicted to *jel-*

lybeans. Nelson Mandela was no terrorist—he was a valiant *freedom fighter.* So, let's bring Nelson Mandela *back*!"

No, I'm not going *to bring him back, John-Paul—Nelson Mandela was cruelly imprisoned for a long, hard stretch of his life, and I'm going to let him rest in peace for the time being. I'm curious, though, as to why you haven't mentioned Britain's Churchill or France's De Gaulle or the revolutionaries Emiliano Zapata, Malcolm X, Che Guevera, George Washington, or Thomas Jefferson.*

"Well, I love the *persona* of Mexico's great Zapata, and Churchill was a leader for the ages—but they were *wartime*—and war*like*—leaders, and *direct hostile confrontation* was where they were at their best. In a *United Empire of Earth,* there should *be* no war. And as for *Washington*—well, he was something of an *elitist,* and he even *owned* lots of *slaves.*"

John-Paul scratched his head in deeper contemplation.

"Maybe You could raise Vladimir Lenin or even Abe Lincoln or Haiti's Francois Dominique Toussaint L'Ouverture the way Your Mystic Son Jesus Christ is presumed by the faithful to have resuscitated the fallen Lazarus. I appreciate Your professed confidence in me—*truly* I do—but this job appears to be *monumental* to the point of being far beyond my *capability*!"

John-Paul scratched his head again.

"Or perhaps You should consider bringing back Helen Telford, a smart and saintly kindergarten teacher I knew well (who also happened to be the unlucky mother of the miscreant misfit *John*—with whom I happen to have the dubious distinction of being rather *too closely* acquainted).

"Hey, I've got it! Maybe you could bring back Karl Marx—or else *Groucho* Marx—Groucho was a pretty smart guy, You know."

Groucho Marx?? I can't believe *you're actually daring to* joke *with Me again! You'd better* watch your step, *John-Paul.*

"Actually, that wasn't really a *joke,* Your Godliness—grouchy old *Groucho* was an extraordinarily resourceful guy. His kindred comedic spirits Joan Rivers or Robin Williams maybe could do it too. Their recent tragic leave-takings were a great loss to all humankind."

The old poet scratched his head yet again; then suddenly he snapped his fingers: "*Hey,* this time I've *really got* it—how about bringing back *Jesus*?"

I'm not going to bring any *of them back—not even* Jesus *(at least not right now).* Jesus *is a Topic for another time.* Sitting straighter in Its phantom chair, the prepossessing Presence appeared to John-Paul to have somehow suddenly become significantly *larger. I* told *you,* It boomed, *that I'm the Lord and Creator of* all *humankind—not just the Christians*!

"Well, then, if Your Godliness is declining to bring *any* of them back—or Mohammed, Confucius, Lao-Tze, or the Buddha, *either*—how about having someone who's still *alive* head it up? How about Benjamin Netanyahu or Anglican Archbishop Desmond Tutu, for instance—or maybe Bill Maher or Whoopie Goldberg, or Presidents Barack Obama or Jimmy Carter or Bill Clinton? Or *Hillary,* maybe? Or possibly visionary Senator Bernie Sanders?

"Or perhaps *better yet*—the brilliant john a. powell, the University of California-at-Berkeley professor who uses no capital letters in his name. I seriously doubt that powell's loquacious old teacher John Telford could do it, but maybe his *cousin*—my good friend *Jeffery* Telford—could. Jeffery, a retired Ford Motor Company executive and the son of the late Frank Telford, a brilliant but volatile and Left-leaning Hollywood producer-director in the 1950s and '60s, is highly intelligent *despite* inexplicably and stubbornly remaining a *confirmed Republican.* Jeff has often told me that he would *love* to perform a role similar to the Emperorship of Earth (although I do fear that he might deal too harshly and indeed rather *ruthlessly* with slimy governmental or corporate transgressors). All of them except Tutu and Carter are younger than *me*—and Obama's *far* younger—so their mental acuity may well be sharper than mine is at my advanced age."

No, John-Paul. You're *my man, and you must accept that.*

Even though you're eighty years old, you still retain all of your cognitive faculties. You've also learned from life *because you've suffered emotionally and sometimes physically for most of your life, your chronic womanizing and addiction to philandering are behind you, you're in fairly good health, you still retain a youthful storehouse of audacity and nervous energy, and you're still totally committed to winning. You were a successful boxer and a world-ranked sprinter, and you are therefore familiar with the physical risks and sacrifices that championship-level achievement in such a heightened and rarified atmosphere demands. You also learned hard lessons as an incarcerated teen and later got expelled from a high school for misbehavior. You have a heart that is filled with a love of justice and egalitarianism and your fellow man and for children and helpless animals, as well as for the weaker sex of your wayward species.*

Moreover, even beyond My familiarity with your poetry and your other writings, I am very well aware of your liberal proclivities*:*

You've withstood bullets being fired into your home at midnight when you were aggressively recruiting black administrators in an all-white school district, and you've withstood death threats when you were bringing hundreds of black students into another all-white school district. You've fought those whom you call "white supremacist fellow-travelers in blackface"—top black officials in a big, overwhelmingly black *school district who were criminally exploiting the very children they were supposed to be educating.*

You have also been liberally *indiscriminate in your romantic involvements. You dated black and Asian and Latina and Greek and non-Chris-*

tian women long before it was "fashionable" or sometimes even safe *for someone of your ethnicity and inherited creed to do so—and late in life you intrepidly endured seven tumultuous years of marriage to a flat-out "drama queen" of African origin.*

I therefore know that you will do right by all *of My creations on Planet Earth—not just the ones favored by their wealth or their fortunate circumstances of birth or race or creed or ancestry or their willingness to compromise their integrity or by just plain dumb good luck. Know that I am familiar with another little couplet you wrote:*

'We who put conscience *above our* careers
Are dying as a breed, and are deep in arrears.'

Hearing all this, John-Paul spontaneously felt the need to do something he had never done before: He got to his bare knees on the hard cement walkway beneath the grayish-purple cloud in which he knew the Presence hovered, and he cried out: "*Then*, Your Deified Infiniteness, I'm at Your *service*—but You must tell me how I am to *accomplish* all of these things! This is all so new and overwhelming, and I need You to know that I'm filled to overflowing with absolute *trepidation*."

Do not be afraid, John-Paul—and let not your heart be troubled. I am with you always, even unto the end of the Earth. Throughout your long and stormy career, you have been characteristically blessed with great tenacity *and* audacity*, as well as a fearless* veracity *when others in the education profession "ducked down in the weeds" and took the easy, opportunistic road and dissembled and "*went *along to* get *along." With Me and Truth and Righteousness always at your side and always in your heart, you will not fail: You* cannot *fail.*

In your Christian Bible in Romans 1:20, it is written, "For the invisible things of Him since His creation of the world are clearly seen, being perceived through the things that are made—even His everlasting Power and Divinity."

The Voice of the Eternal Presence then took on a deeper, booming sonorousness:

John-Paul Jones the Third, via My everlasting Power and Divinity, I am infinitely certain *that in your heart of hearts you have always known that I exist. He Whom you Christians worship as "My Son" and your Divine Shepherd was indeed the Christ—a great* Teacher*—but* I *am the* ETERNAL *Presence. I am Alpha and Omega, the Beginning and the End—and I also am that mystically* Un-Beginning End WITHOUT End *that you cited in one of your more paradoxical and metaphysically challenging poems. I am the ONE PERFECT AND INFINITE INTELLECT Whose Existence all members of your species sense, and long to know.*

And soon now, through you*, all of them* will.

John-Paul Jones the Third rose to his feet. "My Lord God, I now must believe in Your Existence and in Your Infinite Power and Perfection. I pray that You will guide me and tell me how to do your bidding, for I still don't entirely grasp what is *happening* to me."

I shall*—but first let Us ensure that you know the things that need to be done to rescue this planet and its inhabitants whose arrogant and power-hungry human "leaders" have so direly trashed and endangered—and that you fully understand the reasons* why *these things must be done.*

Let's assume that you were United States President Barack Obama*, for example, and that I had given you—as the Emperor of Earth—this charge to save the world: Which tasks would you undertake first?*

"Well, Your Godliness, were I Barack Obama, who currently is the President of the United States of America and now would theoretically become Your anointed appointee as Emperor of Earth, I first would need to find a *means* to make my fellow Earthlings aware that I have suddenly come to *possess* this God-given power. Then I would help them understand *why* I am doing what I am doing. Finally, I would have to find a way to make them fully aware of the *consequences*, should they balk at conforming with Your divine will, which I will be imposing here on Earth in Your Holy Name."

You're beginning to get the idea, John-Paul. We will discuss the means *and the* consequences *in a later conversation. Be assured that you may well need to get some DSA (Divine Supernatural Assistance) from Me to help you make them both happen—and if and when that Help becomes necessary, as it probably* will, *I promise you that My DSA will definitely be forthcoming.*

Right now, though, I'm immediately interested in hearing you recount the tasks you think that you *(not* Obama, *but* you*) will need to undertake.*

"O Divine Presence, then hear me: Things are happening in my home town of Detroit and my home state of Michigan that threaten to destroy my city, my state, my nation, the entire ecology of the world we live in—and thus ultimately *humanity itself*—if these things are allowed to continue and advance unchecked. I see the prevention of these things as the tasks that I will need to undertake first."

Tell me about these things, John-Paul. You have my undivided attention. Go on.

"I *shall*, Your Godship: Our state has become a *testing ground* for what greedy corporate interests have in mind for the *rest* of our country. Detroit—its largest city—is their target, and its schools have been the 'bull's eye.'"

Elaborate *on that, please—and you're going to need to give Me some concrete examples.*

"Well, one example lies in the fact that Detroit's public schools were taken over by a Republican governor in the year 1999 under the guise of 'reform' simply because he *could*. At the time, DPS enjoyed a $100 million surplus, and its student test scores were at the state midpoint and rising despite the city's many social problems. However, Detroit voters had passed a $1.5-billion bond millage to build some needed new schools and renovate older ones, and the Governor, his cronies, and his masters—the voracious corporate crocodiles and gangster *banksters*—were eyeing with avaricious eyes the resultant contracts to be let.

"A decade later, the schools' gubernatorially appointed 'emergency manager' departed and left behind a $327-million deficit and test scores that were the worst in America. His successor gave away fifteen of those schools—including five high schools—to a gubernatorially created so-called 'educative' quasi-school district euphemistically named the 'Educational Achievement' Authority that failed grievously to educate *anyone*. I dubbed it the 'Educational *Apartheid*' Authority because it was a product of the neo-Jim Crowism that has become endemic in our state. It's a long and ongoing story—but since then, the schools have *further* degenerated."

Yes, John-Paul, I know—*the socio-political crisis of twenty-first century Detroit and Michigan and indeed to a near-equal degree of all* America *is in a very real sense an* intellectual *crisis. From the K-12 schools' and indeed the* universities' *lack of* purpose *to most of their students' lack of* learning, *and from the jargon of "liberation" to the supplanting of* reason *by "creativity,"* American democracy *has unwittingly played host to vulgarized concepts of nihilism—as* relativism *disguised as* "relevance," *and indeed disguised as so-called* "tolerance." *American youth* in general *lack a knowledge and understanding of human history, so naturally they also lack a clear vision for the future. Detroit youth in particular are not only economically impoverished—they are* intellectually *impoverished as well—and across your entire nation, this indeed is also generally the case not only with* black *students but with* white *ones, too, in the overwhelmingly* white suburbs *as well as in the overwhelmingly black and brown* cities.

In the New Order I envision for Earth, ethics-based Philosophy *and the* Liberal and Poetic Arts *will supercede the physical sciences in the curricula from kindergarten through graduate school. Kant and Spinoza and Marx and Hegel and Sartre and Shakespeare and Milton and Plato and Diogenes must in a certain sense precede even* Einstein. *Far too many presumptuous* scientists *today seek to deny* My creativity *and My* power *to work* miracles *as an unproved or even* disproved *theory of the distant past. Still,* human creativity—*which is a mere* pallid imitation *of* Mine—*has in the field of* Philosophy *degenerated to an* unthinking conformity *to democratic* public opinion. *That democratic* public opinion *has been sacrilegiously* misled *and* misshaped *by some academic pseudo-philosophers'* 'Romantic' notions *going way back to the eighteenth century "Age of Enlightenment"—notions that were adapted to* flatter *that* public (every man *a so-called "*Creator*!").* I *am the only* true *Creator.*

But I interrupted you. Give me more examples of the immediate tasks you believe you will need to undertake in your new role as Emperor of Earth.

"Well, Your Godliness, first let me say that—given Your ability to perform physical miracles at will and as needed to make all these wonderful things happen—I agree with You about my putting the liberal and poetic arts in a precedent or at least an *equal* position to the physical sciences in this impending new global empire You desire."

He deliberated for a moment and then observed,

"In order for me to give You examples of the things I will have to address first, I need initially to continue to describe to You some conditions of a *local* nature. As Your Godship in undoubtedly aware, like the situation with Detroit Public Schools, the city of Detroit itself is under 'emergency' management that has been nearly a total failure as well. There was a time as late as the first decade of this century when I thought that a process called 'Federated Regionalism' potentially could fulfill the dream of obliterating racial segregation and the resultant economic inequities that have been so extraordinarily instrumental in fueling the violence in Detroit. Federated Regionalism is a metropolitan model devised primarily by Detroit native son *john a. powell*—now a professor at the University of California at Berkeley. It is a process wherein the large regional authority controls access to opportunities while the lesser authorities control issues of local identity and governmental responsiveness. In predominately minority communities, it establishes provisions for the residents' full participation. Its prime target-'projects' become the majority-white suburban communities that are basically driven by majoritarian motives and therefore often behave with abject self-interest. *Self-interested* local control too frequently becomes *exclusionary* local control. With Federated Regionalism, more attention and funding are applied to improve *urban infrastructure* rather than to provide new capacity for *suburban expansion.*

"Federated Regionalism could have worked for metropolitan Detroit, but it was never applied. The lot of the ordinary citizen has worsened horribly in Detroit. During this summer of 2014, the city's EM actually shut off the *water* going to many thousands of homes in the city because jobless, impoverished homeowners were unable to pay their water bills. Since March, 2014, officials under the administration of the Governor's appointed Emergency Manager have shut off the water for 17,000 Detroit families who owe more than $150 or are two months behind on payments. (They even shut off the water of some families that *did* pay!) A single mother living in the blighted Brightmoor neighborhood in northwest Detroit was keeping a jug of water by the toilet for flushing after they shut off her water. She took a shower when she picked her daughter up at a relative's home.

"And speaking of *water*—on August 11, 2014, metro Detroit suffered what will be millions—no, perhaps *billions*—of dollars' worth of damage from a terrible rainstorm that had drivers nearly drowning in hundreds of submerged cars on the freeways because state legislators haven't fixed the outdated drains. They've been afraid to raise the needed taxes."

John-Paul paused for breath, and then plunged on:

"The powers of the democratically elected Mayor and City Council have been in effect *suspended.* Detroit's Emergency Manager appointed by the Governor has all the power. The Detroit EM has pushed for a declaration of bankruptcy, but he has spent *$75 million* of Detroiters' tax money in *high-priced attorney fees* to foster this so-called 'state of bankruptcy.' He thus used our own tax money *against* us. A Democratic city that elected Democratic leaders is now controlled by the appointee of a Republican governor. *Half* of the state's *entire black population* resides in Detroit. So through this state takeover, half of all black Michiganians have lost their constitutionally guaranteed right to vote meaningfully! City agencies and entire school districts with predominately black populations have been outsourced or privatized. Public employees have been laid off in droves. A state-of-the-art school for *severely handicapped children* and one that actually taught students to *pilot aircraft* have been closed. Art and music instruction have been virtually eliminated. Municipal leaders have sold off or given away vast stretches of public land to corporate interests. City employees have seen their contracts whittled down to nothing. Detroiters are victims of a free-market experiment in which the consequence is speculative interests resulting in profit.

"Meanwhile, a former city councilwoman who now teaches *government* (!) at Wayne State University actually made the unfeeling statement, 'If those people want *water*, they can jolly well go down to the *river* with a *bucket*!' Can you *believe* that? It recalls to mind Queen Marie Antoinette's callous remark of two centuries ago. When told the people of Paris had no bread, she said: 'Then let them eat *cake*!'

"In Detroit, an old former laborer on Social Security disability whose roommate is in a wheelchair (partially paralyzed from a random gunshot) has limped on a cane down the street every day since the shutoff with a bucket to get water from a neighbor's outdoor spigot.

"Thousands of Detroit children and sick oldsters with bedsores have been unable to be bathed or to wash themselves, cook their food, flush their toilets, take baths, or have water to drink. Your Godship, it is clearly a *crime against humanity.*

"Another example is this so-called 'war on drugs.' Detroit is a horrifying textbook case of what is also happening throughout the United States. In effect, the 'war on drugs' has cost hundreds of thousands of lives and created a new class of people who have lost their rights and have become objects of persecution and racial discrimination."

Yes, my son. I of course am aware of all of the situations and conditions you describe, and I share your related concerns that you have so eloquently expressed in your poetry. I do agree that if these illogical and unfair conditions were to be left unchecked, they would continue to contaminate your entire country with pervasive injustice and tragedy. That is why I have enlisted you to help Me fix *these kinds of things in America and throughout the planet.*

Also, know that I too *fancy Myself a Poet when the mood takes Me, to wit:*

Fascism & Classism

Fascism & classism
Are clearly nearly the same crime.
Therefore I say that since they may,
They clearly nearly need to rhyme*!*

Fascism and classism are "isms" *that are natural kin to* Nazism, *which first raised its monstrous head in Nazi Germany two years before you were born but in fact* has no geographic borders, *as illustrated by the conditions you so eloquently cite. Tomorrow I am going to ask you to share with me some of your concerns that impact not just Detroit and Michigan but the greater population of your nation—and which therefore will eventually affect the whole world as well.*

With that, the Divine Eternal Presence lifted the entire expansive cloud cover and disappeared swiftly into the fourth dimension. The still-rising sun shone again brilliantly upon the lake, dancing on the waves in countless sparkling points of light.

Roy Reeves, John-Paul's next-door neighbor to the north, emerged at that moment from his house in the waning coolness of the morning to walk his two dogs along the water's edge—one a friendly old retriever and the other a large female Bouvier named Strawberry that had repeatedly demonstrated that it didn't like John-Paul.

"Hey, neighbor," Roy said, as Strawberry growled worrisomely at John-Paul, "Where'd you get that remote control that can drive your boat? I saw what you *did* yesterday. Really, couldn't that be kind of dangerous? And is it even *legal*?"

"It wasn't a 'remote control,' Roy," said John-Paul, as he eyed the big Bouvier nervously. "In actuality, I asked God to drive my boat in that little circle out there to demonstrate that it was truly He Who has been speaking to me, and now—since I saw Him *perform* that miracle—I know for sure that He in fact *has* been speaking to me."

Roy chuckled. "*Right*, John-Paul. Okay, neighbor, you don't have to tell me where you got it, if you'd rather not. But that sure was some *unlikely* sight out on the lake yesterday!"

It was at this moment that John-Paul Jones the Third realized that convincing neighbor Roy of God's new Plan—and acquainting everyone else out in the wide world with God's Plan as well—was going to be far from easy.

Lost in thought, he opened the gate and walked back across his long lawn into the sun room at the back of the house and went into the kitchen. For a few minutes, he stood and looked out the window at the miles-wide expanse of Lake St. Clair. Above that backyard window of his and Balalaika's house and hideaway, the short porch portico shaded the glow of a white, ascending sun, as the huge lake became an endless sea of silver under a pearl-colored sky. Like that rising sun, the stark realization began then to dawn on him that convincing the world of his *own* Divinely anointed and impending role in *effecting* God's new Plan was going to confront him with perhaps the greatest challenge of all.

IV.

On the *third* day, God rested.

On the *fourth* day, at eight o'clock in the morning, He/It intoned to John-Paul, who had just finished his breakfast and was about to take his extensive heart medication and his daily thyroid and prostate pills,

All right, old man—you've rested enough *now, as has your Deity. Let Me hear some more about* how what is happening in the American State of Michigan *will impact the rest of the world for the* worse*, in your opinion.*

John-Paul gulped down his eleven morning pills, looked out his kitchen window up toward the sky, and announced in a loud voice to the Great Eternal Presence, Which he presumed to be somewhere up there nearby on high,

"O Great God, I want You to know that I've begun to *agree* with You about *democracy*: Our government in this country appears to be compromised and split and broken almost beyond repair. I never really thought so until now, but I've lived to see Nixon and the two Bushes and Dick Cheney and the turncoat Clarence Thomas and the current fascistically inclined governor of my state, who has imitated Hitler by suspending human-rights laws and putting *oberfuehrers* in municipalities whose populations are predominately citizens of color.

He calls them 'emergency managers,' but they're really *oberfuehrers* similar to those that Hitler installed in the provinces after he was *democratically* (!) elected to the position of Chancellor of Germany in the early 1930s. He then took over the schools and the press, as the Michigan governor is evidently also doing. Hitler's next step was to assume control of the SS (*Schutzstaffel*) and the military—and *that* was *all she wrote*. The Michigan governor rules a state, not a nation—but he does command the State Police, who function as an occupying military force on Belle Isle, Detroit's great island park which the state has commandeered against the wishes of grass-roots Detroiters."

Don't even mention six of that gaggling gang of seven *to Me.* Four *of them will be relegated to the dustbin of history one day—not to mention the fires of Hell—and* two *are in there already.*

"I understand, Your Godliness—and *believe* me, I agree with you *entirely* about those four treasonous traitors to democratic ideals—and particularly, of course, about Adolf Hitler. I hope that monster—that slimy snake from Hell—is back down there frying within the depthless torches of eternal hellfire right this very minute—after the horror of the Holocaust he engendered.

"I even wrote a *poem* about him once, affecting a German accent in the poem. I titled it 'Adolf THE Adder':

Reichsfuehrer, 'schieskopf' Schickelgruber,
vas hatched a *schnake* from Hell.
I vish *schummvunn* had *schtumbled* on it
And *schtomped* it in its *schell*!

"Did Your Godship know that 'Schickelgruber' was that *scheiskopf* schithead Hitler's—er, I mean that shithead *Hitler's*—real name?"

Of course *I knew it—I know* everything. *And I must say that that's a cutely clever little quatrain you penned with all of its* 'schtumblings' *and* 'schtompings'—*but John-Paul, you once wished for Hell to be a* myth! *You can't* have *it* both *ways.*

Remember this other *poem you wrote, which I will now quote back to you –*

Dante Andante, *or Dante Denied*

In our lifetime journey's journal
Man's un-Heavenly Inferno
May not be somewhere external:
Hell could truly be internal.
Though we tend toward errant turning,
And we're slow to lesson-*learning,*
Yet we yearn to never burn in
Someplace evil and Infernal—
And Hellaciously eternal.

You did *write that poem, did you not?*

"Yes, Your Godliness, You *know* that I did. But in that first poem—the 'Schickelgruber' one—I used the hypothetical concept of 'Hell' *figuratively*. As for the *other* poem—let me say that I have always imagined that the exact location of Hell may not *be* external—off in the outer stratosphere somewhere—or far down deep in the Earth's bowels, as depicted in Dante's epic poem *Paradise Lost*. Rather, given some of my own agonizing life experiences and similar ones of millions of my fellow humans, I have imagined that perhaps *Hell* could well exist in our own tortured bodies and psyches right here on the surface of bad old *terra firma*—and thus hopefully and prayerfully, not *everlastingly*. I hope and pray that I'm *correct* in this speculation."

Well, John-Paul, all I have to say about that *at this time is that your speculation about Hell is a wise one and an* insightful *one.*

"I have long suspected so, Your Almightiness. However, given my speculation regarding whether Hell possibly is a place right here on Earth, I have also wondered *why* it *is* that for hundreds of years Your Godship allowed more than 100 million blacks to be tortured, castrated, starved, burned, hanged, drowned, terrorized, hosed, chained, sold, murdered, raped, mocked, enslaved, defamed, beaten, mutilated, ostracized, rancorized, segregated, and dehumanized by people who looked like me.

"I have also wondered *why* it *is* that You allowed millions of innocent men, women, and children to suffer horribly throughout the past several centuries in wars, famines, plagues, 'religious' so-called 'inquisitions,' and assorted massacres, 'ethnic cleansings,' genocides, and holocausts. I'm sure that Your Godship is aware that some time ago I wrote a one-word poem entitled '*Shoah*.' That poem of one single word was in the form of an agonized question: '*Pourquoi*?—the French word for *Why*? (*Shoah* is Hebrew for *catastrophe*.) In some philosophic and literary quarters, the word *shoah* has superceded the word *holocaust*. I use the French word for *Why?* in the poem '*Pourquoi*?' to honor Jewish members of the Free French Resistance and (rhetorically) to ask *You*, The Divine Eternal Presence Who presumably controls everything that occurs in the universe, to give us what I (for current *rhetoric's* sake) assumed back then was Your Immortal (but morally reprehensible and mortally *incomprehensible*) reason *why* You have permitted such historic horrors to happen. The brave French freedom fighters of World War II were intrepid examples of *luntsmen* of Jewish boxing champions Barney Ross and Benny Leonard and of their similarly courageous battling brethren in the Warsaw Ghetto. They were all brothers under the skin in a mighty and multitudinous tribe which—far from being slanderously 'destined for martyrdom'—instead produced resourceful warriors who fought the good fight against the Nazis' unspeakable and hideous inhumanity and later re-established a Jewish homeland.

"So I ask You *again* now, straight to Your Holy and Infinite white-whiskered *Face*—*why* the Holocaust? *Why* on *Earth* did You *permit* it?—and *why-O-WHY* did Your Holiness allow those other historic horrors ever, *ever* to *happen*??"

My son, there are things that passeth all human *understanding—and* those *are but a scant few of them.* This *I* will *say: When I gave mankind* free will—*when I granted human beings the power of* choice *and* self-determination—*I opened the door for those horrors* possibly *to occur. With the establishment of your Empire on Earth, I am now* closing *that door.*

The Presence ran an exasperated *faux* Hand across Its anthropomorphically human-like *faux* Forehead.

All right, John-Paul—We've talked enough *about such unspeakable horrors for the time being, amid your presumptuous accusation that I am somehow* responsible *for their* occurrences. *Let's get back to how you think that what's happening in Detroit and Michigan will impact the rest of the world for the* worse.

"Oh, so now You want to *change the subject*? Well, all right, then—I fully realize that *lynchings* and *holocausts* and *pogroms* have *got* to be pretty *touchy topics* for Your Almighty Divinity!

"So, *okay*—I remain most anxious to tell Your Holy Godship how the bad things that are happening locally will have a *global* impact. In fact, I'm eager to *enlarge* upon it, because what's happening in Detroit and Michigan right now could very presently *lead* to horrors like those I just listed that Your obviously *guilt-filled* Almightiness most understandably declines to discuss any further—and perhaps to horrors that conceivably could ultimately be on an even *huger* historic scale, wherefrom I presume You would also wash Your Hands like the Roman bureaucrat Pilate. I've seen corrupt educators and legislators and judges in this very city and in this very state, and I've seen *dumb* ones here and I've seen *drunken* ones here and I've seen *drug-addicted* ones right here, too."

John-Paul was fervently beginning to wish that he had an open and full bottle of *Dewars* or *Johnny Walker Red* in his hand.

"And I've also seen a Michigan governor and his collusive legislators illegally reinstate that emergency manager law in slightly different terminology, even though it is an odious and unconstitutional law that the state's citizens had voted overwhelmingly to *overturn*! That vote itself nearly was prevented from happening, because a Republican-dominated Board of Canvassers initially refused to allow the issue to get on the ballot on the ridiculous premise that petitions signed by a quarter-million Michiganians—not all of them *Democrats*, either—were printed in a font size the board proclaimed to be "*too small*!"

The old poet was beginning to become visibly distraught. Noting this, the Presence said, *You need to calm down, My son—I don't want you to have another heart attack. The Lord knows (with Me of course* being *the Lord) that I am going to need you to remain* healthy.

"I *know*, Your Great Godhead, I *know*—but it's hard for me not to get extremely upset and frustrated when I reflect on the fact that no *federal judge*—or indeed even the *United States Attorney General*—has yet to do anything about *any* of these villainies! I sincerely hope that I'm *wrong* about this, but to *me* the Attorney General appears to be knuckling under to the financial and technocratic crocodiles who dominate Wall Street and Washington. Those pricks think that ordinary workers don't deserve *anything*. Your Godship will note the clear evidence of this in the *Detroit water shutoffs*. I think that the unfeeling authorities have been perfectly happy to cut off water to unemployed Detroit families, because those families will either all *die* from dehydration or *leave*—thus paving the way for a so-called 'Detroit Future City Plan' that is basically the old urban renewal/"*Negro* removal" of the 1960s all over again. The shutoffs weren't designed simply to improve the water system's finances. Had that been the plan, they would be targeting the *corporate accounts*, but they don't want to do that. In order to convince people that this nefarious scheme is legitimate, its architects must lay the blame on the *working class*.

"In Detroit, the emergency manager of the city, who was undemocratically appointed by the dictatorial Republican governor of the state, has filed for that bankruptcy that I told You about yesterday. It wouldn't surprise me to see the Governor declare a state of bankruptcy for the entire county of Wayne, where Detroit is its largest city, and install an emergency manager for the County, which is the state's largest. Robert Ficano—the current Wayne County Executive and an elected official—oversaw scandalous budgetary overruns on a county jail that remained only half-built.

John-Paul, one of the biggest problems with that emergency manager law that you rail about so much is that it is simply a local manifestation of a broader problem—that problem being that your beloved democracy *isn't* working*! It has been suppressed by an overwhelming growth in inequality of wealth and privilege and runaway power.*

"I'm finally ready to concede sadly that Your Godliness may be *right* about the failure of democracy. People are helplessly throwing up their hands because they've watched the *banks* get bailed out, and they've watched their neighbors' *homes* go into *foreclosure*. They've seen their secure future *disappear* right before their eyes. And even when some of them are still misguidedly convinced they can make a difference by *voting*, they quickly realize that their votes do not carry anywhere near the weight that *Wall Street* does."

John-Paul was nearly in *tears* at this point. He blew his nose and pressed on:

"Inch by inch—and then foot-by-foot, yard-by-yard, and mile-by *mile*—Detroiters' long-cherished rights and values have been trampled upon in the name of 'financial necessity.' *Public lands* have been just *given away outright* to developers! The gangster banksters have allowed thousands upon thousands of poor folk in the city to obtain mortgages the banksters knew they couldn't keep *paying* on, and when they missed payments, the banksters foreclosed and took their homes away! The Governor of Michigan has slashed funds for education, taxed old folks' pensions, and rammed through a 'right-to-work' law that he had promised to *oppose.* It is really a right '*not* to work' or a 'right' to work for *slave wages.* Instead of declaring financial emergencies and putting emergency managers in charge in a number of cities—not just *Detroit*—this governor should have used his executive power to declare a moratorium on water shutoffs, foreclosures, and heat shutoffs, and he should have instructed his underling—the municipal emergency manager—to sue the banks. Why is it that we see proposal after proposal to starve the little guy and enrich the corporate ruling class?"

The reason for that, *John-Paul, must by now have finally appeared very* clear *to you: As you* yourself *have told Me, there is indeed an American ruling class with so much money and influence that you can never again have a functioning* democracy *in your country under such egregiously imbalanced economic conditions. This is why I have* enlisted *you and have planned to* help *you establish a* New World Order *that will not depend on the outmoded* Democratic Ideal *to be able to function.*

"Well, I never thought that I'd hear myself *say* this, Your Godship, but now it can't happen fast enough to suit *me.* I now am *Your man, indeed.* Why, outlandish tax breaks have indeed been allotted to developers in Detroit, while old people have indeed seen their pensions *taxed* and *slashed*! Citizens have been threatened. Hundreds of thousands of people have lost livelihoods, homes, and health care. Hundreds of once thriving public schools have indeed been closed right here in the city under our very noses. Classrooms in the schools that remain far exceed 40 students *contractually*! This is totally unacceptable. And while the Detroit Public Schools' 'emergency' management was supposed to bring 'business-world efficiency' to the public schools, spending on central administration has now actually comprised a larger slice of the pie than ever before. It's close to impossible for teachers to teach successfully in such disgracefully overcrowded classrooms.

"Does Your Godship need to hear still *more* of my mewlings and rants?"

Absolutely—and I see that you're warming *to your testimony.* Continue *it.*

John-Paul took a deep breath and plunged on:

"Political cronies line their pockets while abusing our children in for-profit 'academies' designed to deaden imagination and creativity. A candidate now has to raise and spend more money in this state—as well as in *any* state—than the actual *annual salary* of the office he seeks! On a 5-4 decision, the United States Supreme Court has incredibly and illogically adjudged that *corporations* are *persons*, so they can be undemocratically enabled to donate limitless amounts of money to corporate-collusive candidates. In 2013, my own state legislature ruled that now no one has the right any longer even to be able to find out who's putting out the big money to brainwash and deceive the electorate."

He took another breath.

"And let's not forget that most of the very few fortunate black men in Detroit who *do* have good, steady jobs still make far less money than their white counterparts. This same racial imbalance in wages and salaries exists in the suburbs, as well—and this very same discriminatory imbalance is actually true everywhere in the U.S."

Balalaika, who had awakened and crept downstairs, overheard her husband. "Yes—and *women* earn less than *men* do for the *same work*," she snapped. "Make sure you also tell Him *that*. Also, if you're going to be a good Emperor of Earth for *all* of your subjects, I also want you to make sure that some *schools* get named after Alice Paul and Martha Griffiths. They were the ones who insisted that women's issues get under the tent of the civil rights movement, since its chicken-shit leaders have been reluctant to let that happen."

Your wife is absolutely right about the wage inequity, John-Paul, And she's also right about the key roles that Alice Paul and Martha Griffiths played in getting the women's movement piggy-backed onto the movement for rights for African-Americans. Please tell her that the ancient God of her long-suffering Jewish forefathers is painfully well aware of all *of that.*

John-Paul glanced impatiently again at Balalaika. "God said he already *knows* that, Bala—and He also wants you to know that He is the true God of your fathers—*Jehovah* and *Yahweh*, I believe, are two of the names He *went* by with your forefathers.

"And now, if you want to stay downstairs here in the kitchen with me, I want you to keep quiet so I can concentrate on giving Him my answers that He has asked for. Otherwise you're going to have to go back upstairs or retreat to the living room."

God sternly interrupted him:

I don't want you to tell *her that, John-Paul. You mustn't* banish *her—she will be your* Empress Balalaika *and as such will have a key role in the coming* Empire of Earth. *You're going to have to get used to communicating with Me directly* anyway *in the presence of your top lieutenants—who actually will be your feudal kings and nobles—both in the fifty states of America and also in the various other nation-states that will now become part of your world empire.*

God furrowed Its *faux* Michelangelan brow. *And know that your Empress will be one of your key consultants—as well as—along with* Me, *of course—your* conscience *at times, as needed. Be* clear, *though—and make it clear to* her*—that I don't intend to permit anyone except you as the* Emperor of Earth *to experience My Presence either aurally or visually.*

"Godliness," John-Paul asserted, "Your *wish* is of course my *command*, although I fear that at the outset of my Imperial reign many people will indeed think that 'the *Emperor* has no *clothes*'—You are of course familiar with the parable to which I refer, with *me* having to play the role of the 'naked Emperor' in this instance."

John-Paul turned then to his wife and informed her solemnly, "Balalaika, God says you are to be my *Empress* and are therefore entitled to listen to what I say to Him. However, I still need you to remain silent during my conversations with Him so I can *concentrate.* What is happening at this very moment in our lakefront kitchen right here on Jefferson Avenue in this tightly insulated little town of St. Clair Shores is a truly historic turning point in all of human history, even though no one out there knows about it yet."

You've definitely got that *right, John-Paul,* God said. *But the rest of the world is going to know about it all too soon, as well. They soon will see that the Emperor most definitely* does *indeed "*have clothes*."*

And now*—do you have any other concern of a* local *nature that you need to communicate to Me before you tell Me your perceptions regarding your greater global tasks that must be undertaken to get your empire up and running?*

"Yes, Godliness, I do. I have friends and relatives who visit me here to swim and fish, to ride with me in my speedboat, and just to schmooze. For example, Alvin Ward, the athletic director of the Detroit Public Schools, comes out here in his rare spare moments to fish in this huge lake which You have abundantly filled with fish (although he never seems to catch anything even though he brings a whole trunk-full of fancy equipment). I also like to drink with that old scatological author/poet John Telford's cousin Jeff up in his tree house on Oxbow Lake in White Lake Township on warm summer days like today—and at my suites on the Detroit River on some fall and winter afternoons. Will I still be able to spend time with all of those folks to do those relaxing things in those places?"

Of course *you will—Nixon had his Bebe Rebozo, Henry of England had his Falstaff, a certain Prince of Wales had his Beau Brummell, Victoria had her Master of Horse—the Scot John Brown, and so on. Incidentally, regarding the* latter *liaison: I must caution you that the one thing that I will strictly forbid you is any involvement of a sexual nature with anyone other than your Queen-Empress Balalaika. It is My firm and uncompromising belief that marriage and total monogamy within it represent perhaps the best of the historic Judeo-Christian traditions.*

"I have no problem with that, Your Godliness, at this stage of my life. Actually, I no longer have either the inclination or the capability to consort with multiple females."

*All right—I'm very glad to hear you say that. A*lthough the Presence had chosen not to appear to John-Paul in any visible form during this particular conversation, the old activist educator detected in Its tone an element of relief—and even the slight trace of a Divine *smile*. *You know, John-Paul,* God added, while still indeed slightly smiling, *Allan Bloom is one of My favored Earthly philosophers, along with Confucius, Aristotle, Nietzsche, Rousseau (sometimes), Hegel, Voltaire, Goethe, Freud, and Thomas Mann—and also Martin Luther, Reinhold Niebuhr, Wayne Dyer, Edwin Rowe, Father Tom Cunningham, and Prof. john a. powell. Allan Bloom once quoted* Nietzsche *as having said that* writing a poem *could be as subliminally erotic an act as the actual engagement in sexual congress. In that spirit, I wish you ongoing bliss in* both *activities, insofar as you no longer* over*indulge in* either of them—*since* governing the Empire of Earth *must now become your primary concern.*

I am also aware that you as a poet, artist, and musician sold paintings and won fiddling, poetry, and foot-racing competitions: Thus, I expect you also to be the Empire's foremost artistic, cultural and recreational *leader. I presume that you will place Plato over Dr. Phil, favor Alexandre Dumas over Grace Metalious, choose Itzak Perlman over Mick Jagger, Beethoven and Lizst over Guns 'n' Roses' "music" and acid rock, Robert Frost's iambic pentameter and tetrameter over Fifty Cent's hip-hop and rap, Raphael over Warhol, boxing (f you* must*) over cage fighting, soccer over football (particularly for pubescent males), track & field athletics over stock-car racing and tractor pulls and demolition derbies, swimming competitions over hydroplane racing.... You get My drift.*

So*—John-Paul, do you have any* further *local concerns, before We turn to your* global *ones?*

"Yes, Godliness, I do—but they involve the *how* rather than the *what.*"

As I said, the how*—that is, the* means*—will be addressed later.*

I'm going to let you rest just a bit more for the next couple of Earth-days while I extinguish a minor conflict that some lower creatures of My creation have become enmeshed *in near the midpoint of the universe. Upon My return, you can begin to recount your global concerns for the task ahead.*

God's Voice was beginning to fade ever so slightly, and John-Paul knew that He/It was about to leave the scene.

After you have shared your global concerns with Me, John-Paul, you and I will then discuss the how *that We have been contemplating—following which you'll need to gird yourself for the initial* local *and very soon thereafter* global battle *which immediately shall follow....*

Having uttered those fading words (that incidentally *traumatized* the worried John-Paul considerably with their allusion to impending local and global *battles*),

God the Great and Divine Eternal Presence was gone.

V.

"Your Great Godly Goodness," Jean-Paul began, when God the Great Eternal Presence returned two days later to resume their dialogue, "I confess I don't know where to start, since I have so *much* to say about national and world problems."

Well, my son, the Divine Presence offered helpfully, *then just dive right in at the middle and cut to the chase!*

"All right, Your Godliness, I will:

"African-Americans have been killing each other every day in our big cities. Syrians have also been killing each other in Syria, Iraqis have been killing each other in Iraq, Libyans have killed each other in Libya, and Hutus and Tutsis are gearing up to kill each other in Rwanda again. Palestinians and Israelis have been killing each other, and Americans and Afghans have been killing each other. Ukrainians and Russians have been killing each other over the Crimean dispute—and the rebels there also shot down and killed hundreds of innocent passengers from several countries on a Malaysian plane that was flying harmlessly over the murderously embattled Ukraine."

Jean-Paul paused for breath.

"Totalitarian regimes possessing nuclear weapons in North Korea, Pakistan, and possibly Iran present potential threats to world peace, as do China, Russia, and a number of former Soviet states.

"In the face of all this global conflict, the American president and Congress have unwisely decided to reduce the United States' military force to pre-World War II numbers. They are about to lay off 87 experienced career captains and majors and thousands of enlisted men.

"As a new round of violence kicks off in Israel/Palestine and more children and other civilians are killed, it's not enough to call for yet another ceasefire. It's time to take definitive non-violent action to end this decades-long nightmare. Our global governments have failed—while they have talked peace and passed United Nations resolutions, they and our own domestic corporations have continued to aid, trade, and invest in the violence. Al-Qaeda, the Taliban, Hamas, and the genocidal *Isis* all train terrorists and recruit suicide bombers all throughout the Middle East. Now they're even recruiting and training some Jihadist Brits and immigrant or first-generation Middle-Eastern-Americans.

"More specifically, we must find an immediate means to stop Isis' torture and massacres and beheadings of the Kurds in Iraq and the hellish cycle of Hamas firing rockets at Israel, Israel bombing Gaza, and daily decimation of innocent Palestinian families. Archbishop Desmond Tutu of South Africa—one of our truly great non-violent leaders—has pointed out that we should be helping to create the conditions for a lasting peace between Israel and Palestine, and safe homes for Jews and Palestinians alike. Both anti-Semitism and discrimination against Palestinians—like all hatreds—are grotesque and must be eradicated. It is the extremists on both sides who endanger a peaceful future for their people."

Balalaika, who in addition to having been a teacher was also a retired Detroit public-school principal, had wakened and come downstairs, and she had listened to John-Paul's words to the Divine Presence raptly, her gray-green eyes wide in fright.

"My husband," she whispered, "You must ask God to neutralize everyone's nuclear weaponry immediately—including *ours*—before someone starts the Third World War.

"Please tell Him, too, about the recent revelation that the CIA is actually spying on our own Congress—and that is not an isolated incident. I was reading the *New York Times* yesterday, and in trying to explain the damage inflicted by this wrongdoing, the editors of the *Times* stated, 'It is all of Congress—and by extension, the American public—that is paying for an intelligence agency that does not seem to understand the most fundamental concept of democratic separation of powers.' However, I believe that it's not just the concept of 'separation of powers' that the agency ignores, but our entire *Constitution of the United States* itself and its regard for such individual liberties as *freedom of speech*. The *Times* editorial decries the 'lawless culture' that has festered within the CIA since the moment the war-criminal traitors George W. Bush and Richard Cheney encouraged that rogue agency to *torture* suspects and then *lie* about it.

"Also, John-Paul, you definitely need to tell God about the *rail cars* that can explode while carrying volatile crude oil through America's communities. The United States Department of Transportation needs to ban these hazardous cars before one of them blows up your grandchildren and mine."

"Did you heed my wife, Your Divine Godliness?" John-Paul asked. "I think she just raised three urgent points."

Yes, she did. And she is absolutely right that I will need to take the dangerous nuclear toys out of the hands of your planet's current leaders. Analogically, those men with their fingers on the explosive nuclear button are akin to infants playing in their cribs with loaded pistols or hand grenades with loose pins.

All in good time, *though—all in good time.*

In the meantime, *John-Paul, tell Me* more *about your* global concerns*—and be more specific.*

"Your Eternal Godship, I'm not sure that I can get much more specific than I have already, but I will try:

"There are literally hundreds of absolute dictatorships all throughout our planet—some of them brazenly masquerading as '*democracies.*' As I have intimated to You already, a case in point exists right here in Michigan, which in effect is no longer a democratically governed state. Detroit—which is Michigan's largest and poorest city—is located near two of the five *great lakes* and the Detroit River. It therefore has access to the largest fresh-water supply in the world. I would submit that this *unquestionably* qualifies its rogue governance as a *global concern.* Last year, as I mentioned, tens of thousands of the city's poorest residents were deprived of water when the city's unelected emergency manager began seeking to reduce the Water and Sewerage Department's debt, cutting off residents who are too poor to keep current with their payments. The Department of Social Services then began to take the children and sick old people away from their parents or guardians in some of those households.

"Meanwhile, General Motors and the city's two publicly subsidized sports arenas, which owe the citizens of Detroit countless thousands of dollars in unpaid water bills, have not had *their* water turned off. The democratic rule of law is dead in this state. The United Nations has called the illicit Detroit emergency manager's actions 'a violation of the human right to water and other international human rights.' That most *definitively* makes it a global concern.

"Also, let me add that many middle-class Detroiters who were financially able to do so have pulled their children out of the city's public schools that once ranked among the world's best but are being destroyed intentionally by gubernatorially imposed emergency management, for the economic benefit of corporate interests.

"Was that *specific* enough for Your Godship?"

Yes, John-Paul. Now give Me still more *examples of your concerns—but this time try to be a bit more* global *in their scope!*

"Well, throughout the world, every year billions of pounds of *pesticides* are applied to fields growing foods that human beings *eat*, and the workers who apply the pesticides are the hardest hit by these toxic chemicals. To cite one horrifying example close to home—the men, women, and children who harvest America's food have one of the highest rates of *chemical exposures* among all U.S. workers. Tens of thousands of pesticide poisonings happen to these workers every year!"

Yes, that concern is a crucial *one. Give Me some more.*

"The massive burning of fossil fuels all around the planet is heightening *global warming* to a point of *no return*, lifting ocean levels and threatening low-lying islands in the Pacific Ocean and urban centers such as Long Island and Manhattan Island on our Atlantic coast. It is now eminently clear that Al Gore—from whom the American Presidency was literally *stolen* in the year 2000—was *absolutely right*. This excessive burning of fossil fuels has even threatened to rupture the *ozone*!"

Yes, those concerns are all most urgent ones. Give Me more.

"With Your Infinite Holiness' kind and patient indulgence, I will cite just one more *local* example:

"The current revolutionary/evolutionary/*solutionary* resistance struggles in Detroit and the valiant grass-roots organizing in Detroit—from local food growth and security, to *similar* new work, to the endeavor to establish a new paradigm in *education*, to creating *peace zones* in the spirit of the 100-year-old iconic Detroit visionary Grace Lee Boggs and her late husband Jimmy Boggs—continue to *progress as I speak*. These evolutionary revolutionaries are still attempting to show us an opportunity (and responsibility) to resolve the fundamental contradictions that emerged with slavery from the sixteenth through the nineteenth century. Jim Crow and the imperialist enemies of the Native American ghosts of Wounded Knee have resurfaced in this country wearing fancy tie and tails as '*James* Crow'—a new and subtler but equally insidious form of servitude and genocide perpetrated upon people of color. Slavery by any other name is still slavery.

"These courageous struggles in Detroit, where access to water is no longer regarded as a human right because you have to *pay* for it, but where vast parcels of public land have been given away *free* to billionaires, are being thwarted ruthlessly by those same gangster banksters who sit imperiously in suits and ties in high-rise crystalline monoliths that gleam palatially in the sun. These cruel corporate crocodiles are aided and abetted by hordes of their 'house Negroes' like Clarence Thomas and like some gubernatorially appointed school or municipal emergency managers such as those in Detroit—grinning white-supremacist fellow travelers in blackface, all of whom are kin under the skin to the turncoat trusties at Auschwitz.

"At times, they have also been perceived to march side-by-side with corrupt and/or substance-abusing officials like Washington, D.C. Mayor Marion Barry and the currently long-term imprisoned former Detroit Mayor Kwame Kilpatrick—whose 28-year sentence, incidentally, was nevertheless far too severe, in my opinion. After the passage of the Voting Rights Act of 1965, Professor Manning Marable of New York University and the great black leader Bayard Rustin argued that the American Civil Rights Movement had to shift from Malcolm's direct action and Ghandi's and King's non-violent civil disobedience to activism in the *electoral* arena. Their description of this strategy was 'a *black face* in a *high place*.' Blacks understandably wanted to get people into prominent positions who looked like *them*. They called this 'symbolic representation,' but the problem with that is that it assumes a guaranteed level of *accountability* between the representative and his constituency, and it also assumes that the representative will abide by the law rather than seek a way to *subvert* it in order to *profiteer personally*, as Kilpatrick did."

John-Paul paused, and then he added emphatically, "If the connection is one of mere *phenotype* or *gender* or even *sexual orientation*, those are rather *tenuous* bases upon which to build a *movement*, don't You think? I myself have gradually come to realize this, since even though within the past three or four decades blacks for the first time since Reconstruction have been able to increase their number exponentially in high governmental elected positions which have astoundingly now included even the American Presidency, that has not *guaranteed* nor indeed *resulted in* a particular black (or in *multiple numbers* of blacks) adhering faithfully to the body of politics that initially empowered the African-American constituency."

I see that you're continuing to warm well to your work, and you now are actually illuminating *My Most* Luminous *Luminosity! Go on, go* on!

"I am *warming* to it *indeed*, Your Luminousness! Before You reached down in Your divine and hopefully all-knowing *wisdom* to pluck me from the miserable mass of seven billion humans to be Your Emperor of Earth, I had imagined that we citizens who suffer in America's degenerated *democracy* that has now become a near-absolute *corporatocracy* could somehow mold the blue-collar ranks into a revolutionary yet peacable, mass-based coalition of the *proletariat— black, white, gray,* and *gay*, as depicted in my poem 'Comes the Revolution.' Even if and when the dictatorial emergency management form of government is suspended on constitutional grounds, the material interests behind it remain largely the same. And one maintains this form of rule by intimidating voters, activists, and other enemies of oligarchy."

John-Paul then offered God a few more *concrete examples*: "One actually cannot separate what is going on in *Michigan's cities* from broader national and global trends, whether it be CIA spying on the Senate, military *coups* in countries like Libya, Syria, and Egypt, illegal FBI surveillance in America, or any number of decidedly anti-democratic practices that are being normalized by this era of inequality and instability."

That's all true, John-Paul—nor can any of that be separated from the distorted priorities of your failed national democratic *government, either: The bombs that fall on Gaza* today *will, in a sense and in effect, explode also in your city and in all American cities* tomorrow. *The billions of dollars that your country spends to subsidize wars throughout the world extinguish not only non-American lives, but the hope of a* better *future for* working-class Americans *as well. In your very own words, you have shared with Me that your courts and judges have amply demonstrated that ordinary U.S. citizens cannot rely on them to save you, and your elected representatives have amply demonstrated that you cannot rely on* them *to save you, either. In another of your poems which I need not quote today, you wrote that the time is approaching when* bankers *and* judges *will have to be* held hostage.

Thus, your only chances rest with My Plan! *Again, this is why We—you and I—must do what I am planning for Us to do.*

"Your Godship, in hopeful harmony and perhaps even *congruence* with Your Plan, I'd like to share with You how the progressive thinking of the late Manning Marable paralleled my own. Dr. Marable—who with John Telford, john a. powell, Grace Lee Boggs, Cornel West, and Dr. Wayne Dyer, was tapped by director Joshua Bassett and Wayne County Community College Chancellor Curtis Ivery to serve on the Advisory Board of the WCCCD-District-sponsored Institute for Social Progress—had clearly visualized that same *revolutionary, peaceable coalition* of the *proletariat* which I have also envisioned. Dr. Marable saw it—as I did—not as a formalized party but as a membership organization that would advocate a *progressive public-policy agenda*. Marable saw Humanists, Marxists, and Socialists like me as being able to operate within this democratically-oriented coalition freely, along with gay and lesbian activists, the Gray Panthers, the Anti-Defamation League, the Team for Justice, and black and brown organizations like the NAACP, *La Raza*, the Black Panthers, the Southern Christian Leadership Conference, and the Urban League."

"*Hey*, John-Paul, my *husband* dear," interjected Balalaika with raw, ill-concealed, and long-pent-up emotion, "what about radical *feminists* and the National Organization for *Women*—that egalitararian outfit that Geraldine Barclay leads locally along with some other wise women? Don't forget *them*!"

"Yes, *them*, too," John-Paul added conciliatorily, with genuine earnestness. "Dr. Marable and I both saw this multifaceted coalition—which would include *feminists*, certainly—as being able to campaign for basic issues focusing on public policies and programs involving public education, health care, housing, and more. He felt that this coalition could re-accelerate the stalled liberal movement—the *traditional* one—not the so-called 'neo-liberals' who have sold out to corporate interests. Dr. Marable had long recognized the need for a reconstituted Left and a revived Black Liberation Front. Both would have had to be developed around previously-embraced democratic principles and procedures—but such principles and procedures are apparently going to become obsolete in the Imperial model of world government within which You are planning to have me function as its impetus and Emperor."

John-Paul, there will still be room therein for your expressed concept of progressive public policies and programs, *but (and I am going to say this to you just* one more time*): There will* not*—I repeat,* NOT*—be any room for the* practice *of* DEMOCRACY *in* implementing *them! Humanity has had its* last chance *at* democracy. *Its* faux-*democratic leaders have failed tragically.*

God waited a moment to let that sink in. Then He said, in a kinder tone, *Please continue, though, if you like, to share with Me any other concern you have of a global nature—and I in turn am willing to continue to listen.*

John-Paul swallowed hard and then very foolhardily tried to tout the democratic ideal to The Almighty Presence one *last, persistent* time: "Well, God, since You are aware that I've been a lifelong *Democrat*—both with a capital 'D' and a small 'd'—I still would propose that We find a way to have the various worldwide kings and kings-to-be who will be my vassals in the countries within Your envisioned system of neo-feudalism be somehow induced to rule at least *semi*-democratically, or *partially* democratically!"

Damn *it, John-Paul, were I not* God, *I would take* My Own Name *in* vain *right now! You really* exasperate *Me sometimes. We'll have to talk a whole lot more about that questionable proposition of* semi-democracy *or* partial democracy. *We shall* see *what we shall* see *about any* compromising *on My part in that regard. I am going to "sign off" now—and I'll have to* "sleep" *on it. (I use the term* "sleep *on it" as a figure of Earth-*speech, *of course—because actually, I* never *sleep).*

Tomorrow at noon I'm going to beam you up into one of My celestial clouds again for Us to confab Face-to-face.

"Oh, *wow*—another one of your celestial clouds! That's *great,* Your Mightiness—sitting in the last one with You was sheer metaphysical *rapture.*"

John-Paul paused—and then in a rather wheedling tone he added, "Will You maybe have a *cigar* and this time perhaps some *Grand Marnier* waiting for me in it?"

I'll have a single cigar *for you—and I'll even smoke one* with *you. There will be a glass or two of* old Vernor's Ginger Ale *waiting for you up there, as well—but probably no* alcohol. *We need to get down to* brass tacks *now, and you're going to have to be as* sharp *as one.*

Balalaika had continued to crouch in a corner, carefully listening to the entire conversation, and suddenly she interjected loudly and imperatively, "John-Paul, ask Him if *I* can come up with you and see Him *too*, this time!"

Hearing her, the Presence instructed, *You're going to have to tell your wife one more time again that she* cannot come *with you. She's going to have to hold down the fort there on* terra firma *whenever I beam you up for a confab. I happen to know that she doesn't like to see you* smoke, *anyway—let alone* drink. *And as I have told you,* You're *the* one human being *whom I will* ever *address* directly*—and you must make that crystal-clear to her.*

"All right, Your Eminently Worshipable Divinity—I'll tell her *at once*," John-Paul said with a somewhat smug smile.

VI.

At high noon of the next day, the Eternal Presence accosted the napping John-Paul and again beamed his incorporeal spirit up to a snowy-white cloud with just a touch of very light *gray* in it, while John-Paul's corporeal self continued to nap. The Presence then offered the old man's now fully conscious *spirit* a *lit cigar*, which the incorporeal John-Paul began immediately to puff upon, leaning back in his luxurious phantom armchair and hoisting his phantom feet up on his phantom footstool.

Don't get too comfortable, *John-Paul,* the Presence chided him none-too gently. *I want you to finish sharing your concerns of a* global *nature with Me—and right after you've finished with* that, *we may still have time to discuss some* strategic <u>means</u> *and* <u>matters</u>.

"Your Graciously Benign and Magnificent Divinity, I would like You to know that my next *global* concern will undoubtedly impact upon those very same *means* and *matters.*"

How <u>so</u>, *John-Paul?*

"*Well,* Your Godliness, one of the first things I intend to do as Your Emperor of Earth is use the *Internet* as the vehicle to communicate my Divinely appointed redemptive role to the world and establish my Imperial Government in Your service."

As a matter of note, John-Paul, I had hoped *you would arrive upon that intent without any prompting from your Deity, and the fact that you have now done so confirms that My selection of you to assume the mantle of Emperor of Earth was* indeed *the right choice.*

"Thank You, Your Godship—and I do indeed definitely mean to make full use of the Internet. However, first I will need to enlist Your help to render the Worldwide Web my tool to communicate this information and establish my benevolent government. The Holy American Empire will be partially modeled after the Holy *Roman* Empire of the early sixteenth century, and the United States will resultantly become the major seat of world government, as in essence it once *was* immediately following World War II."

You're saying that your *country is going to be the Imperial Capitol of the Empire of Earth? What about granting* China *or* Great Britain *or* France *that signal honor? Or have you considered Spain, Russia, Iran, Germany, Pakistan, India, Israel, the Netherlands, Mexico, the United Arab Emirates, or other relatively robust powers—as well as perhaps others that are somewhat* less *so, such as Turkey, Iraq, Yemen, Qatar, or Greece?*

Also, what about Syria, Algiers, Jordan, Morocco, the emerging nations in Africa and South and Central America, the Caribbean states, the two Koreas, Vietnam, and several former members of what once was the Soviet bloc? Aren't you being overly ethnocentric to make such a swift and arbitrary designation?

"Yes, Your Divine Greatness, I am. Isn't that what You *expect* me to do?"

As a matter of fact, it is*—I was just* testing *you.*

John-Paul Jones the Third took another growingly confident puff on his phantom cigar. "I realize, too, Your Godship," he said, "that many nations—even those *friendly* to us—will be resentful and probably *jealous*. I worry specifically about the Australians and the Canadians in this respect, as well as the French, the Italians, the Japanese, the English, the Irish, the Welsh, the Cornish, and the fiercely independent Scots, whose younger countrymen currently seek independence from the United Kingdom, and whose ancient heritage I share as a first-generation Scottish-American."

The Divine Presence stroked Its snow-white beard reflectively and said, *At some early juncture, it will undoubtedly become necessary for Me to help you gently nudge some of those nations in the correct direction, and to a lesser extent perhaps to help you nudge* all *of them.*

Tell Me more about your plans regarding the Internet.

"Well, Your Godship, the *wealthiest one percent* of America's population has been seeking to control the Internet *entirely*, along with what everyone else throughout the world will get to *see* on it forever and ever. That would be the 'apocalypse' of the Internet as we humans know it—and if You'll excuse the *reference* I'm about to make, it would erase the *democratic* premise and promise of an information highway for all of humanity. This panoramic, open information highway is what the founders of the World-Wide Web envisioned—and it is the informational thoroughfare that I plan to endorse and build upon."

For the moment, John-Paul, I will *excuse your persistent references to your precious but failed* democratic *"ideal" and your reference here specifically to a* "democratic" *premise.*

I want you to tell Me more *about your plan for the Internet—I confess that your idea in that regard* intrigues *Me.*

"Okay, O Almighty One—here's a *whole lot more*:

"Together, our world community has built on that vision of an information highway for *everyone throughout the world*, using the Web to fight corruption, save lives, and bring people-powered aid to countries in crisis. My own United States as it is presently constituted is on the verge of colluding with the European Union to give the richest corporations the right to *show content swiftly*, while 'paywalling' or slowing down everything and everyone else. To cite two examples: Under these restrictions, a grassroots world-citizen journalist would no longer be able a) to show footage of atrocities in places like Syria, or b) run multinational campaigns to save the grievously endangered ecology of the planet.

"Your Godship, as You and I speak at this very *moment*, high-handed and counter-egalitarian decisions on both sides of the Atlantic are being made by moguls regarding the Internet. As Your impending *benign*, *beneficent*, and *benevolent* Emperor of Earth, I am nonetheless going to be obliged to guarantee a *free and democratic Internet* if I am truly to reign *benignly* and *benevolently* over *all* of my subjects. I know that 'imperial' and 'democratic' are seemingly *conflicting* concepts, but you say that you want *all* humans to be treated *beneficially* and *benevolently*, right? Well, the *democratic ideal* is an *essential component* of that fair treatment! Until now, any improvements in the speed and functioning of the Internet benefited *everyone on the planet.*

"If, for example, Rupert Murdoch's ultraconservative Fox News found a faster way to stream videos, this also benefited the few remaining independent media that have been courageously daring to show the grim reality on the ground in Iraq, Syria, the Ukraine, and Palestine. Politicians call this 'net neutrality,' and laws protecting it used to exist in the United States until a court recently struck them down.

"Now the European-Union Parliament (EUP) is threatening to pass regulations that give these corporate moguls the right to carve up the Web and control *what we can see on it* by *slowing down* or *charging* the sites that don't pay! Web providers like Verizon and Vodafone are lobbying hard for an *Internet for the rich.*

"I intend to ensure that what connects *everyone* stays open, and one of the means I'm going to use to *do* it is one that even *Your Godliness* may not have considered."

Oh, don't think for a sixty-second minute *that* I *haven't considered it, John-Paul.*

"*Really*, O Omnipotent One? If You know what I've got in *mind* here, Your Godship, You're even more *omnipotent* than I thought."

Of course *I know what you've got in mind, John-Paul—you're planning to do away with the* gold standard, *and also eliminate the* World Bank, *right?*

"O Mighty Godhead, You're *close*, but no *cigar*."

John-Paul sat back and took a self-satisfied and somewhat smug puff on his own cigar.

"Your Great Godship, my Utopian Imperial Plan goes far beyond doing away with the gold standard and eliminating the World Bank—I intend to eliminate *all world currency entirely*!"

John-Paul, I knew you were a radical renegade *when I* chose *you, but I confess I didn't know you were* that much *of a radical renegade. Still, I must admit that I rather* like *this* intent *of yours.*

The Eternal Presence rose to Its Michelangelically assumed phantom feet and ran Its Michelangelic fingers through Its long, Michelangelan white beard.

I've got to speed off to the Constellation Ursus Major *now, John-Paul. There's a nagging little skirmish in one of the minor planets there involving* Klingons *that I have to dissolve. I'll be back tomorrow afternoon for you to enlighten Me regarding your proposed* absence of currency *as a component of your Imperial Plan for the Holy American Empire of Earth. Perhaps you should dub it your Imperial Plan for the Holy* Utopian *Empire of Earth, though— because the concept of a* world without money *is a truly Utopian one which even* I *had never contemplated.*

So—I'll see you tomorrow. Ursus Major, *here I come!*

"*Wow*, Your Godship," John-Paul marveled, changing the subject slightly, so impressed was he with the Presence's boast of the speed with which It was able to jet through the galaxies. "Do You mean to tell me that You can get to *Ursus Major* and back in *one day*?"

The Eternal Presence's *faux*-Michelangelic Face broke into a broad grin. *I must confess to you that I often enjoy violating one or more of My own laws—in this instance, the Einsteinian speed limit of 80 miles per second—the absolute speed of light as* theoretically *calculated by that late German-born Jew with the wild hair and the owlishly preoccupied facial expression. I just* love *to soar at speeds exceeding eighty miles per* second *per* second *per* second *per* second *to the Nth degree! I find it to be* most exhilarating.

Later in your global reign, your scientists will have what will now become limitless *opportunities to make myriad* ground-breaking *discoveries, examine and* re-examine *and* prove *or* disprove *literally hundreds of remarkable theories like Einstein's landmark Theory of Relativity, and hypothesize and then* prove revolutionary new ones *that may modify even the brilliant* Einstein's.

And let Me emphasize that this *is the* only *kind of* revolution *I ever want to see occur in your new* Empire of Earth. *No more murderously bloody conflagrations must* We*—you and I—ever again allow to* happen; *do you* read *Me on that count, John-Paul?*

For a moment, the Presence's Michelangelan Countenance had grown forbiddingly stern, but then just a few seconds later it reconfigured Itself again into a beaming, beatific smile.

To utter a deliberate pun, *John-Paul, let Me say that* Relatively *late in human scientists' escalate era of unprecedented social and technological combustion, that marvelous*—nay, *near-*miraculous*—incarnate creation of Mine who went by the Earthly name of Albert Einstein did indeed set forth an incendiary proposition which spun off a sub-theoretical conclusion that time can actually run* backward *as well as* forward *under certain conditions.*

So—John-Paul, I want you to listen carefully to what I am about to say to you, because the best scientists within your upcoming Empire of Earth are going to have to learn to build on this knowledge:

As a few of Earth's most sophisticated scientists and other scholars have even now ascertained, slender strings of pure energy have survived in their original state, rather than cooling off with the rest of the universe after that "Big Bang" that I set off several quadrillion eons ago. Within this cosmic scenario, it is possible for two light rays from a single star to travel by two different paths of different lengths on each side of one of these two strings and end up at the same place simultaneously, *even though it would take one of them* longer *to* get there*—because as that maestro named Einstein conclusively theorized early in your century just past,* light *always has to travel at the same speed. Therefore, the speed of light is the absolute speed limit for anything and anyone else—when it is* mortal *creatures who are doing the traveling by means that they one day shall themselves devise.*

However, any law formulated in the realm of so-called "perfect" mathematics yet and still remains imperfect *in My sight.*

Know ye, John-Paul III, O Divinely appointed *Earthly* Emperor-*to*-be, *that only* I, *The* DIVINITY, *am* Perfect!

Know ye also that following the converse *of this particular law, if I so chose, I could travel in time and arrive back here* yesterday *instead of* tomorrow! *I just* love *to explore ways to transcend "natural" laws which I Myself have set forth as* absolutes, *because that's the* only *kind of puzzle that an Omnipotent Entity like Me can create for Myself to muse over and ponder upon. To find paradoxical ways to break My own unbreakable laws is a refreshing challenge that I like to pose to Myself. Being the One and Only Almighty Deity in the entire infinite universe, I get quite lonely sometimes out there in the cosmos, so this is sort of like having an Alter Ego with Whom I can amuse Myself.*

And as I said, I often do *choose to follow* no law at all, *whether it be Mine or Mendel's or Einstein's or Euclid's or Newton's or Pascal's or indeed* Murphy's*—and whether it be obverse, converse, or omni-verse!*

Having thus so articulately and Divinely spoken, the Great, Divine, and sometimes strangely *lonely* Eternal Presence vanished from John-Paul's sight with disconcerting abruptness, and the once-again fully corporeal old poet found himself stirring slowly awake from his noontime nap on the sofa in his sun room facing the lake.

He got up, donned shorts and sandals, a hat with the words 'Detroit Track & Field Old-Timers' emblazoned on it, and an orange "Detroiters Resisting Emergency Management" tee shirt. Then he told Balalaika that he was heading over to his friend Jeff Telford's place, climbed gingerly into his bashed-in, black 2008 Lincoln Town Car, and backed it out of the garage.

His wife ran out and asked him, "How'd your latest afternoon session with the Almighty go?"

"You know, Bala, I actually felt a little *sorry* for Him today. He bears a vast and solitary cosmic burden. I'll tell you more about it when I get back."

"Tell me about it *now*. And you weren't planning to go to Jeff's house looking like *that*, were you? You're wearing the same wrinkled shirt you had on yesterday. Get back in the house and change your shirt. Also, brush that stringy long hair of yours. It looks pretty greasy, too—you really need to wash it."

“Oh, yeah—I guess I forgot to brush it.” John-Paul took a do-rag out of his shorts pocket and wrapped it around his head.

“John-Paul,” Balalaika screamed at him, “take that goddamned ridiculous *handkerchief* off your head!”

“You’d best not take the Lord’s name in vain, Bala—He’ll *hear* you.”

With the wrinkled do-rag still atop his head, shirt unchanged, and hair unwashed and strings of it sticking together, old John-Paul the Poet turned the car around, pulled out of the driveway onto Jefferson, and headed for M-59 and his friend Jeff’s place.

Later on that same day, Balalaika invited the recently widowed Sarah Carnahan, the Joneses’ 75-year-old next-door neighbor to the south, to come north around the fence separating their large lakefront yards and partake of some snacks and conversation while John-Paul was away drinking and smoking *Antony y Cleopatra dark* cigars up in Jeff Telford’s imposing tree house in White Lake Township.

When John-Paul arrived back home, Balalaika told him, “I let Sarah know a little bit about what God has in store for you, and right after that she excused herself rather abruptly and went into her huge house and didn’t come out, even though today is a bright, sunny day—a good day to stay in her flowery yard or in ours. She didn’t say anything about what I shared with her, either, but I’m very much afraid that her uncharacteristically strange behavior was because she may think I’m a little ‘touched in the head.’ Should I *not* have told her about your very real and genuine pact with God?”

Yes-you-should-*not*-have-told-her, Bala,” John-Paul said, irritably mimicking his wife in a sing-song tone.

“Still,” he added, “I don’t think that God will care whether or *not* you told her. God—the *Lord*, the *Great Eternal Presence*, the *Great Spirit in the Sky*, or whatever other name we might call Him by—in His

Divine Infiniteness *infinitely* understands how *infinitely* hard my task is going to be just to get Earth's vast human aggregate to understand and believe that the things that God wants to happen via my *imperial* and *imperious* decrees will really and inevitably *happen* that way, and that I miraculously am somehow to be the *catalyst* for it as well as the *emperor of* it!"

John-Paul paused for a moment to study her probingly. "I'm not sure. though, whether even *you* fully understand yet that everything is going to have to happen in precisely that way, Bala."

He sighed deeply, then smiled and gave her a hug. "What do you say we take in a *movie*? I don't know about *you*, but *I* could *really* use some R & R right about now. So far, this apparitional 'Eternal Presence' and Its 'Empire of Earth' scheme have been absolutely overwhelming, and—to paraphrase the popular old song title—'it's only just *begun*.'"

VII.

The Great and Divine Eternal Presence did not return the next afternoon as It had promised. Its "nagging little problem" in the Constellation *Ursus Major* had become more *major* than *minor* and had unexpectedly delayed It. It wasn't until three days later that the Presence *presently* was *present* back on Earth, sounding an immediate and shrilly clanking, clamorous alarm inside the metal plate in John-Paul's weary head and waking him past midnight from a fitful sleep.

He and Balalaika hadn't taken in a movie, either, as they had planned to do three days previously. She had forgotten to bring her cell phone and had gone back in the house to retrieve it and had slipped and fallen backward down the stairs from the garage to the kitchen, breaking her left arm, which was the one she favored. John-Paul had rushed her to Emergency, where the doctors put her arm in a cast. The break was in the ulna, the smaller of the two long bones in her forearm, and the pain had kept both her and her husband wide awake for most of the two previous nights.

Thus, the first words out of John-Paul's mouth to the Presence were, "Your Godship, my wife Balalaika has broken her left arm, and she's *left-handed.* I've had to bathe her, apply her deodorant, undress her, and dress her…and she has been in terrible and debilitating pain for three days. "Can You heal her arm?"

Of course I can, my son. The Presence gestured in a sweeping half-circle with the spread Fingers of one phantom Hand.

There! *It is* done. *Go downstairs now and get those tin snips out of your kitchen drawer and cut off her cast. Then go back upstairs to your office and shut those two folding doors. We've got some serious and very* fast *talking to do—not* Balalaika*—just you and Me, without any of her time-consuming interruptions. I want to get the control of the World-Wide Web into your hands quickly—before your country and the EU* [European Union] *render it a needlessly* complicating *nuisance for Me to do that.*

The Presence's gaze narrowed. *And let Me add that I* apologize *for costing Us those three unexpected days, but it couldn't be helped.*

John-Paul lost no time following the Presence's instructions regarding cutting off Balalaika's cast and rushing back upstairs and shutting the folding doors to his office. He was well aware that he and the Presence would need to move quickly regarding the World-Wide Web, as he was certain that remote corporate moguls interacting with each other in Calcutta, London, Paris, New York, Los Angeles, New Delhi, Berlin, and Washington, D.C. had already given their technicians orders to initiate the reservation and restriction of the fastest conduits of the Internet's information highway to the richest one percent of the American and European populations, as well as to elite chosen (and nearly equally well-heeled) others around the planet.

All right, John-Paul, God the Eternal Presence said to him, *give Me a very* brief *synopsis of your plan for the elimination of currency in your imperial plan, and I'll let you know now whether I approve it. Make it really quick, if you can, because We are confronted right this minute with pressing matters that demand Our immediate attention.*

"O Infinite Master of Eternity's Innumerable Horizons, first let me thank Your Infiniteness for healing my wife's broken arm. She, too, gratefully thanks You, for her pain was near unbearable."

Yes, yes, *John-Paul—you're entirely* welcome. *You had to* know *I would do that, of* course*—now get down to addressing the business at hand. We don't have a lot of time.*

"Well, then, with Your Godly permission, let me make this quick reference to an idealistic tome entitled *Utopia*, penned in our Earth-year 1516 by Sir Thomas More. In More's centuries'-old book, Utopia is a socially, politically, and economically idyllic but *imaginary* island. In my imperial global plan, Utopia will be imaginary *no longer* when this planet that we Earthlings call our 'Earth' becomes a truly Utopian 'island' in space."

At this point, John-Paul took an extremely deep breath and began to talk very fast:

"In order for me to achieve the establishment of this idyllic state of Earthly affairs, it is my intent, with Your Godship's leave, to decree that all *currency* of any kind be declared extrinsically *valueless* in all nations. In its place, I intend to set up my world-wide Resource-Driven and Technology-Driven Economic System (RDTDES). This economic mechanism will represent the ultimate evolution of the most advanced form of *true Socialism*—the Utopian system of social organization wherein the vesting of the ownership and control of the means of production, capital, and land is entrusted to the community as a whole.

Under My Plan, it will indeed be Utopian, John-Paul, but it won't be Socialistic. That smacks of Marxism, and England during the latter part of the first half of the twentieth century had a great essayist named Eric Arthur Blair whose pen name was George Orwell. In his allegorical novel Animal Farm, *he pretty well illustrated how that can't work. Karl Marx was a brilliant human with some excellent ideas, but his overweening premise was proven flawed because humanity* <u>itself</u> *is grievously flawed, I'm sorry to say. Nonetheless, Utopianism—as Plato the Greek tried to teach your species at the outset—*is *the* <u>fire</u> *with which you have had to* *play because it was the only way human beings have been able to discover who they are.*

"Yes—Plato wrote a timeless book titled *The Republic* which I was required to read in college. While a 'republic' is a nation where the citizens are sovereign and vote for representatives to carry out their wishes, a certain unprogressive and obstreperous American political party that uses the *elephant* as its symbol has grossly corrupted the word."

So have many corrupt members of a certain American political party that uses the ass *as* its *symbol—and it in turn has grossly corrupted the word "democracy"—but go on.*

"Well, I do realize, Your Godship, that within Your Plan, this will be an all-encompassing *Imperial* system, rather than a Socialist one, or a pure democracy. Yet even so, I as its impending Emperor envision it to be one in which every citizen in the Empire of Earth will be enabled to participate and to which each and every one of them will be able to contribute an artistic, poetic, legislative, legal, medical, musical, governmental, judicial, horticultural, hygienic, dietary, or literary service in a profession or vocation in accordance with his or her aptitudes and skills, *multi*-skills, or *semi*-skills.

"And those with *no* skills or aptitudes of any kind at all will still be completely cared for by their fellows.

"Also, in my Imperial society, all of these skills will be seen as having *equal value*, whether the skill be that of a *plumber* or of a *heart surgeon*—because society needs *both*. Cooperation and the sharing and pooling of natural and manufactured resources, goods, real estate, and artistic and technological talents and services will abound globally.

"The currency-based job-system we have operated under for centuries offers too *much* to some and *little* or *nothing* to others.

"It depends on production for the sake of *production* and consumption for the sake of *consumption.*

"It compels unequal relationships between the *employer* and the *employed.*

"It is *cruel* to the *unemployed.*

"It drives the insatiable *destruction* of precious natural resources.

"It is hostile to the creation of *community.*

"It is inherently stressful to *individuals, families* and the *greater society.*

"It grotesquely *deforms* the entire process of *education.*

"It politically empowers *some* to the unfair disadvantage of *others.*

"It reproduces entrenched *racial* and *global disparities.*

"It promotes *conflict* rather than *cooperation*: As currently structured, the global *currency*-based job system is not only *failing*—it is a *menace* to life on the planet. It is a system whose time now will blessedly be *past.*"

At that point, John-Paul's tone became very intense. "This will all transpire," he asserted, "amid the permanent banishment of *war*, which even in the immediately recent time before Your Coming to anoint me as Emperor of Earth had become at least *semi*-obsolete on a purely practical basis, given the Pandora's Box of nuclear weaponry that was opened forever in 1945. This remains true even though some benighted so-called 'leaders' of nations haven't realized it yet—nor, I fear, have many of their hair-trigger-happy military commanders grasped it, either."

Fingers spread in supplication, John-Paul gestured skyward toward the Presence with both hands.

"Your Godliness, the love of (and dependence upon) *money* is indeed the Biblical 'root of all evil.' Both presently and historically, it has engendered gross and egregious inequities among men. For example, in our present unfair economic system, Africa can produce perfectly viable and nutritious agricultural goods, but farmers in Europe and the United States are paid subsidies that enable them to sell similar produce at giveaway prices, wreaking havoc upon African countries' economies and upon other poorer countries' economies throughout the world. In my RDTDES (Resource-Driven and Technology-Driven Economic System) that I intend with Your Divine leave to set up in the impending Empire of Earth, there will be no World Bank and indeed no *money*, nor would anyone need any. All we would need are *each other*."

Well, John-Paul, I asked you to give me a very brief *synopsis—and that verbose one which you just gave me I estimate contained five or six hundred words and thus was fairly far from being* brief.

But yes*—you have My Divine leave to engender a* moneyless *regime. I think it's a tremendously innovative idea that I should have envisioned Myself.*

Now I want you to get some rest and then take your wife to that movie *you missed. It's still* playing. *In the meantime, I am going to draft an Internet communication for the World-Wide Web and run it by you before it goes out. Tomorrow at your Earth-noon in another hemisphere of your planet, I'll be spiriting you up in a cloud again to review My drafted document. Perhaps, too, I will have a chilled glass of Grand Marnier waiting for you there this time.*

And you are right *when you say, 'All we would need are each other.' Given the nearly limitless greed and related weaknesses of your miserable species which has become a poisonous parasite upon your planet, your idealis-*

tic, Utopian plan to initiate your Resource-Driven, Technology-Driven Economic System would never *work in an* ordinary democracy—*nor indeed even in a* traditional monarchy *or* dictatorship. *However, in this new* Empire of Earth, *where* you *will be the benign Emperor and* I *the Enforcer, it has the potential to become an Eden for your subjects—an Earthly facsimile of the Elysian Fields or even of your Biblical* Heaven.

I look forward to tomorrow with singular anticipation. I feel like dining *on* LIGHTNING *and* bending THUNDERBOLTS! *I can truthfully say to you, John-Paul, that your Ancient and Omnipotent Deity literally hasn't been this* galvanized *in* EONS!!

VIII.

The next day at high noon over North Africa in a gigantic cumulous pink-and-white cloud eight hundred feet above Cairo (*Egypt—not Illinois*), John-Paul's temporarily disembodied spirit sipped the heady, orange-based liqueur from the glass that God had just handed him and smacked his spiritual lips. He smacked them again when he finished reading the unrolled parchment from God that he held in his happy phantom hand. Arching his back in his phantom armchair like a pleased and contented cat, John-Paul in his spirit form took another sip of the Grand Marnier and smacked his lips a third time.

"Your Mightiness, this Holy Scroll is a rare work of not only *literary* art, but *visual* art, as well!"

In the lower right-hand corner of the crisp papyrus-like parchment was God's seal in vivid red wax with the white-bearded Michelangelic Image affixed to it in a large disc of what appeared to be clear plastic—the *ancient* melding with the *modern*. In the lower left was a smaller color photo of a bejeweled-crowned John-Paul in the same clear plastic upon green wax. Etched upon the parchment in ornately curled black letters in bold Old English script, as from the quill of a medieval scribe, was this long and portentous introductory sentence:

Family of Man, let it be known throughout all the mountains, across all the oceans, and beside all the hills, rills, rivers, valleys, and plains of your bounteous planet that **I**—*your Great, Gracious, and Eternal God—do* *this Earth-day in My Infinite Wisdom baptize and anoint King John-Paul III of America to be your Omni-Earthly Emperor and reign over you in peace* **forevermore** *with My Divine Blessing (and also* **well within the Terrible, Swift Sword**-*reach and range of My Personal and Perpetual* **Protection**).

This celestial message to all humanity went on to spell out the essential Imperial Edicts which would presently become absolute law throughout the world, to wit:

Eighty-year-olds would remain *eighty* forever; twelve-year-olds would remain *twelve* forever; infants would remain *infants* forever. There would be no more war or killing or wife-beating or molestations of children or old people or animals. God's message advised bankers and bank employees that very soon permanent padlocks would be materializing as if by magic upon the doors of banks throughout the planet, and He advised all heads of state and their generals that all weapons of war and killing would hereby be rendered useless upon human flesh, and that bombs could no longer explode. It also spelled out the Divine *punishment* that would be meted out to anyone who attempted to violate these new Rules and Commandments as set forth by the Eternal Lord.

It was signed *God the Father*, in a big, bold, Michelangelan Hand.

What do you think of my logo, the Eternal Lord God the Father asked of John-Paul. *Is the* beard *too* bushy*, perhaps, or not* white *enough?*

"No *way*, Your Godliness. Were that perfectionist artist who so sublimely painted Your Image on the high ceiling of the Sistine Chapel alive today, even *he* would have to pronounce it '*perfect*!' Mine *eyes* have seen the *glory* of the Coming of the *Lord*!" John-Paul drained his glass and grinned at God exultantly.

Yes, indeed—thine eyes truly have *seen My glory, My son. And John-Paul, do you know what? I almost wasn't going to tell you this: For variety's sake, and as a nod to racial equality and feminism, I had planned at first to use the personified image of a* black woman *as Myself on this logo and really blow the male chauvinists' minds down there—and I did indeed initially take on that Apparition—but then I tried out an accompanying suitable Voice to address you that just didn't have the right timbre of* sonorousness, *so I switched Myself back to* Michelangelo's *Version of Me.*

"Well, I've got to say that I'm really rather glad You did, Godliness, John-Paul said in a tone of undisguised relief. "I've got to confess that the concept of a *female* '*God the Father*' just doesn't quite *cut* it with me."

Yes, I sort of figured *it wouldn't, you* male chauvinist, *you!*

Fairly soon, too, I—in your preferred Michelangelan Image of God the Father—will indeed be "stamping out the vintage where the Grapes of Wrath *are stored," because hundreds of thousands of these parchment Scrolls are going to materialize miraculously on the desks of every head of state and of every big corporation president and bank president and newspaper publisher and college president and school superintendent throughout the entire world, with an elegant red ribbon neatly tied around each of them. They will be rendered in English where English is understood, and in other languages as needed.*

The Scrolls are also going to materialize on the desk of every general, *every* admiral, *and every* police chief—*and at the hand of every* terrorist leader.

Simultaneously, the same message will appear on the Internet *over My Image and yours.*

Very soon, all hell *(if you'll pardon the expression) is going to break loose down there!*

"Glory, glory, hallelujah," John-Paul exclaimed. "Glory, glory, *hallelujah*! The old-time, all-time *righteous crusade* as celebrated and sung in the stirring old 'Battle Hymn of the Republic' is *really* and *truly* on the imminent horizon!"

Yea, verily, *my son—it* is *imminent indeed.*

The Great Eternal Presence glanced out Its glassless window and down at the Pyramids in the distance through a break in the drifting cloud-cover and remarked, *Over your lake back in southeast Michigan today, there were no clouds anywhere* close *to being this majestically magnificent, so on a whim I spirited you around the planet into* this *one instead. We'll head back* to *your* hemisphere *now.*

The Presence snapped Its long Michelangelan fingers and *presto*! – They were immediately sitting in Their chairs in an almost identical cloud high above the deepest point of Lake St. Clair.

"Wow," John-Paul marveled, looking down at the lake through a break in this new cloud. "That was really a smooth, fast ride. It must be wonderful to be God and be able to do all these incredible things."

It's not always as great as you might imagine, My son. With great power comes great responsibility, as you will soon learn.

"Your Gracious Godship, if you'll pardon my saying so, I think that I have learned it to a significant extent already. Throughout my career as an activist educator, I have been directly responsible for the education of thousands of students, and *indirectly* so for tens of thousands more. Many times during that long career, I have undergone persecutions from racists, Arab-haters, Jew-haters, homophobes, and other assorted bigots for doing what was right for *all* of our children. Oftentimes, those persecutions cost me even higher-level jobs and caused me repeated grief and hardships."

Yes, I know that, John-Paul. Still, in many ways, your impending tasks are going to be much easier for you throughout the coming millennia than your humanely educative tasks were for you then, and most of yours will be far easier for you now than most of Mine have ever *been for Me.*

During the time of the Civil War in your country and the two great and terrible World Wars on your planet, I fell into a deep and less-than-Divine melancholy.

I fell into an even deeper depression during your Vietnam and Iraq wars, because unlike the Second World War, for example, they were unnecessary and senseless, fought under false premises. Following the Vietnam and Iraq wars, I saw your nation sink into a quagmire of bribes and corruption at the highest levels of state and national government. It was then that I came to My final grim and reluctant conclusion that democracy *just doesn't* work *for humankind.*

"And yet, Your Godship, You said that You are going to grant me permission to utilize *some* democratic precepts, practices, and principles in my reign as your duly anointed King of America and Emperor of Earth, did You not?"

Yes, John-Paul, I did—but I did not say that with total finality*. In that regard, I also told you that we shall* see *what we shall* see, *remember? Despite the quadrillion concerns—both major and less major which I'm currently monitoring elsewhere in the universe—I'm going to need to be the close Monitor of the situation on Earth in that respect.*

"All right, Your Gracious Godship, and I *welcome* Your Monitorship. However, since in Your Godhead's own words my reign is to be 'benevolent and benign'—*democratic egalitarianism* must almost *perforce* be part and parcel of that equation, wouldn't You say?

John-Paul, perhaps you still aren't hearing *Me, so let Me say it to you just* one more time*: In regard to the possibility of retaining any* remnant *of* democracy *in the New World Order,*

We shall need to see *what We shall* see.

IX.

God the Great Eternal Presence had predicted that all *hell* was going to break loose when His/Its Holy Scrolls mysteriously appeared through locked doors as if by magic on the desks of the heads of state and the other moguls and military leaders across the planet—and *break loose* it did.

In Washington, Barack Obama—the resourceful and ordinarily fair-minded American President—got on the phone in bemused haste and ordered the chief of the CIA to prevail upon the Michigan Governor to order the Emergency Manager of Detroit to order Detroit Mayor Michael A. Dublin to have the Detroit police chief arrest the so-called "Emperor" John-Paul Jones III at midnight in his primary residence at the River House on East Jefferson Avenue in Detroit.

John-Paul was handcuffed, whisked to Detroit City Airport in a police car, and flown on a military plane directly to Guantanamo, the American base in Cuba, to be interrogated—praying plaintively and despairingly to the absent Presence all the while, "Your Godship, *do* something! *Do* something!! Why-O-*why* hast thou forsaken me?"

The President also ordered that any staff member who had access to the Oval Office be brought in and questioned in an effort to determine who had planted the mysterious Scroll on his desk.

All around the planet, various other leaders had issued similar orders regarding *their* offices.

Back in Detroit, at orders of the FBI director, Balalaika had also been taken into local custody and held for questioning in the Wayne County Jail without being allowed to make the customary *one phone call* to Robert Plumpe (pronounced *Plum*-pee), John-Paul's and her friend and attorney. Plumpe himself had also been picked up and held incommunicado for questioning for a full week before being released. During the week he was incarcerated, his main concern was the wellbeing of his two grossly overweight and pampered male sibling cats. However, both of them were even healthier when he returned, having been quenching their thirst out of the toilet bowl the entire time while he was gone—and also having lost some weight which they had badly needed to lose.

The FBI also came very close to detaining Detroit Mayor Michael Dublin, who had spent time with John-Paul at John-Paul's place at the River House and at his hideaway on the lake during Dublin's campaign for Mayor when he had succeeded in obtaining John-Paul's endorsement for his candidacy. The Mayor had also appeared on John-Paul's radio show. So, of course, had Democratic gubernatorial candidate Mark Schauer, who—not being the smooth, fast talker that Dublin was—got hustled in handcuffs to an undisclosed location by the Michigan State Police at the Governor's orders. He wasn't released until the President himself interceded on his behalf.

Several friends and neighbors of John-Paul and Balalaika at their places at the River House and at the lake had also been picked up and held briefly for questioning, including lake-side next-door neighbors Sarah Carnahan and Roy Reeves and his wife Ruth.

So had some of the Imperial couple's relatives, including their children by previous marriages—and in the case of John-Paul, by a liaison that hadn't involved a marriage.

So had Balalaika's previous two husbands and John-Paul's previous two wives, plus an indeterminate number of his multitudinous previous known paramours.

His first wife, Marilyn—whom he had cheated on chronically for 28 years—told the officers who questioned her, "He's a rank *subversive* and a *Socialist*, to boot. He's probably also still an *adulterer*—leopards don't ever change their spots. I hope you lock him up for the entire duration of his natural life and throw away the *key*!"

His second wife, Tina, a still relatively young-and-pretty African-American, told them, "Remind Grandpa that I warned him something like this would happen to him some day if his old white behind didn't stop his crazy crusading for our cause. The creaky codger is getting way too *decrepit* for that sort of thing."

Seven of his former ladies who were married and had also happened to be wed to their same husbands during the course of their relationships with John-Paul claimed to not only have never been in an intimate liaison with him, but in three cases actually claimed to never have been even *acquainted* with him. Unfortunately for the verifiability of all of these claims, the authorities had turned up considerable evidence to the contrary consisting of old motel records and the testimony of frightened friends of the claimants, so some of the husbands concerned resultantly initiated divorce proceedings.

When Balalaika kept insisting that her husband was their *Emperor anointed by God* and that they had damn well better let him go *at once*—and that they had *double-damn well better* release *her*, at once, *too*—they whisked her off kicking and screaming to Washington, D.C. and checked her into a psychiatric ward there incommunicado, for "appropriate therapy."

At Guantanamo, meanwhile, interrogators were keeping John-Paul in a glaringly lit room, depriving him of sleep, and asking him again and again and *again*, "How did you manage to get that so-called

'Message from God' onto the World-Wide Web? How? *How*? You'd better tell us how you did it, Dr. Jones. If you don't tell us, we're going to have to resort to some measures that you're not going to like."

"*I* didn't do it, damn it—*God* did it! How can I make you assholes understand that? And I'm *telling* you, I don't know *how* He did it. I'm not a 'techie' by any stretch of the imagination. I can't even hang a fucking *picture* straight! God knew that it would be absolutely fruitless for Him to even *try* to explain to me how He was going to do it. He just *did* it, don't you *see*?"

"All right, John-Paul, if you're going to continue to insult our intelligence with these ridiculous fairy tales, we're going to have to take sterner measures with you."

The head interrogator turned to his assistant. "Ralph, take him to the waterboarding room."

"The *waterboarding* room?" John-Paul shuddered. "Why has God forsaken me? You bastards, you *can't* waterboard me—I'm an *American citizen*, and I've committed no crime. Waterboarding is contrary to the regulations of the Geneva Convention, and it's a form of *torture*, despite what that corporate-collusive dickhead *Dick Cheney* said. "It's also *unconstitutional*!"

Blithely ignoring John-Paul's protests, the agents dragged him crying, praying, and cursing to the waterboarding room—but when they approached the waterboarding apparatus and were about to immerse him in its tortuous treatments, a very strange thing happened:

It vanished entirely, into thin air.

Everyone in the room just stood there transfixed with astonishment except of course John-Paul, who raised his gaze toward the sky and shouted "Yes!! *Thank* You, O Great and Indomitable God! *Thank* You!"

Then an even *stranger* thing happened:

John-Paul's entire living, breathing physical *body* with its eternal soul intact *within* it was divinely and miraculously *dematerialized* from the grasp of two agents who were still clutching him.

He became instantly *re-materialized* sitting in his lakeside kitchen in his favorite chair, still feeling tense—yet also at once *relieved* and absolutely *exultant.*

Tenths-of-seconds later, God dematerialized the Empress Balalaika out of the Washington, D. C. psychiatric ward and similarly re-materialized her into her own chair beside her husband in her lakefront kitchen...

...and a familiar deep voice then resonated boomingly inside John-Paul's head:

You really didn't think I was going to let them <u>torture</u> *you, did you, Your Imperial Majesty?*

The next order of business for Earth's New World Order is going to be your assembling your country's royal government and then approving or replacing the heads of state in the rest of the nations within the Empire of Earth. At some early point along that continuum, you will be crowned King of a new America and Emperor of Earth at the foot of the Lincoln Memorial in Washington, D.C.

*Very soon thereafter, you will embark upon your glorious and peaceable reign over your global Empire of Earth, to the everlasting benefit and joy of all forever-*old *and forever-*young *and newly* <u>immortal</u> *humanity!*

X.

Even before the coronation of Emperor/King John-Paul III at the foot of the Lincoln Memorial with the invisible Eternal Presence beaming benevolently down from the highest peak of a great, gray, gathering storm cloud, John-Paul had publicly named Balalaika his *Empress/Queen* and recent U.S. President Barack Obama his acting *Prime Minister* for America. (He conferred the second of these eminent honors despite both *his* and the *Presence's* reservations about Obama's having done little or nothing as President to prevent the corporate siege of Detroit and the takeover and privatization of its public schools, as well as of other ones throughout the nation.)

He had also conferred upon the recent U.S. senators the titles of 'Duke' or 'Duchess' and upon the recent U.S. Congressmen the title of 'Marquis'—including, somewhat grudgingly, the *Republican* senators.

The three officials who had been in charge of the U.S. Territories of Puerto Rico, Guam, and the Virgin Islands he had named 'Viceroy.'

Passing over the title of 'Viscount' for formerly elected mid-level governmental officials because of its implication of *subordinateness*, he had conferred upon U.S. representatives the title of 'Baron.'

He had then pronounced the governors of the fifty states 'Grand Dukes,' although he had to swallow hard to do this in his home state of Michigan because of his negative views regarding its recent Republican governor, Rip Sniper, who as Governor had appointed and presided over undemocratic school and municipal emergency managers throughout the state. John-Paul had mimicked Sniper regularly and mercilessly on his Sunday afternoon radio shows ("...well, Governor Sniper, you're really quite tough, / And I'm learning that even you *nerds* can get rough— / So now we'll induce you to free up our schools / From 'emergency' management, run by your rules / And your *puppet*, who recently handed away / Some fifteen of our schools to the failed 'EA'A." [The initials 'EAA' stood for Educational Achievement Authority—that pirate outfit which John-Paul had earlier derisively dubbed the "Educational *Apartheid* Authority]).

Drawing upon his familiarity with the titles and protocol of the historic English aristocracy, King John-Paul III of America had also conferred the title of 'Earl' or 'Countess' upon the men and women who had previously been the county executives of particularly large American counties. In the case of old, squinty-eyed L. Brooks Badderson of Oakland County in Michigan, he again had to swallow hard before conferring upon that arrogant and elitist hardline Republican this honorable title.

He awarded the title of 'Baronet' to the mayors or managers of sizeable American cities (except for Mayor Mike Dublin of Detroit. Due to the soon-to-be-crowned King's personal friendship with his new hometown Mayor, he had somewhat whimsically conferred upon the capable Dublin the alliterative and loftier title 'Duke of Detroit.' He had done this despite worrying just a tad that this title might swell the Mayor's already notably swelling head to a size too big for his hat.

He had shown no such favoritism to the city councilpersons in Detroit or throughout the country, though, naming them simply 'Knights' or 'Dames.'

After that, he had conferred the title of 'Esquire' upon lower-level officials in the state governments.

Yielding in two cases to incipient nepotistic proclivities, he had also pronounced his 50-year-old son Steven and his 42-year-old daughter Katherine and her children to be 'princes' and 'princesses,' which titles he had also conferred on his engineer godson Richard ('Rick') and his teacher goddaughter Joy and their offspring, and on Richard's and Joy's mothers Virginia and Barbara, and on Balalaika's daughter Gina by a previous marriage.

He did reverse himself and decide to hand out Viscount and Viscountess titles indiscriminately to some of his friends, including retired Berkley (Michigan) High School principal George Blaney, activist Michael "Doc" Holbrook, his attorney Robert Plumpe, Detroit Technological Institute Professor Rhoda Stamell, and old-time, longtime lady friend Judith, plus an additional handful of his former wives or girl friends who were still alive, and Lamar Lemmons III, the president of the Detroit School Board, for whom he had worked as the school system's *pro bono* superintendent for a year before being fired illegally by its Emergency Manager.

In something of an afterthought, he had even added Roy Robber, the former emergency manager who had fired him, to this list of those who were to receive the title of 'Viscount.'

Robber was a 76-year-old retired General Motors vice president with a huge ego, and King John-Paul was planning to install him in a nice but somewhat less ostentatious house and convert his 20,000-square-foot dwelling in Bloomfield Hills to a theater for showing free vintage Hollywood films and old newsreels of Detroit-area track & field athletes such as Olympians DeHart Hubbard, J. K. Doherty, Eddie Tolan, Lorenzo Wright, Hayes Jones, Henry Carr, Rex Cawley, Darnell Hall, and Lauryn Williams winning their Olympic medals. The old/new king figured that the old former auto executive would need at least to have an aristocratic *title* of some sort to avoid becoming overly depressed in the new American kingdom where this eighty-year-old king intended that *this* time the meek were *really* going to inherit the Earth.

It should be noted that these 'Viscount' awards hadn't made God overwhelmingly *happy*—particularly the *Robber* one—but still He had indulgently allowed all of them to happen, simply because His Divinely anointed appointee to the newly created American throne had *wished* for all of them to happen. God felt that since John-Paul had been His choice for the job, the old Poet King should be allowed some leeway in how that same old Poet King *administered* it.

King John-Paul also *poetically* decreed that his late paternal grandparents and his late parents be posthumously declared "Kings and Queens *Emeritus*" in two separate, formal, and extremely solemn pre-Coronation ceremonies, and he invited prominent American poet M. L. ("Mike") Liebler, who subsequently became Poet Laureate of the Kingdom of America, to compose a poem to read for each of those two occasions.

In thus declaring that his deceased father John-Paul Jones the Younger and deceased grandfather John-Paul Jones were posthumous '*Kings Emeritus*, John-Paul would be crowned *King and Emperor John-Paul III* instead of being crowned King and Emperor John-Paul I.

A midnight incident in early August of 2014 that occurred prior to John-Paul III's coronation attracted world-wide attention. Some members of a South American drug cartel crossed Lake St. Clair from Canada in a small boat, climbed onto John-Paul's and Balalaika's wrought-iron dock, crept ashore, and attempted to assassinate John-Paul in his bed before he could take over his global empire and put a permanent end to the exploitation of the masses by drug cartels and other corporate moguls—illegal and "legal." The would-be assassin who tried to shoot John-Paul died instantly from his own bullet when the Presence reversed it in midair by Divine cosmic remote control and sent it plunging backward straight between the man's eyes into his cerebellum, as Balalaika screamed loudly and then presently calmed down enough to call the St. Clair Shores Police Department on her cell phone.

John-Paul held the two other deeply traumatized would-be assassins at pistol-point until the police arrived.

Another minor incident a week later involved a small Cessna that a lone Taliban suicide pilot who had entered Canada with false papers and had attempted to fly across the lake to crash into John-Paul's and Balalaika's lakeside bedroom at two o'clock in the morning. At the vigilant and protective Hand of God the Eternal Presence, the little airplane fell from the sky into the water off the western shore of Lake St. Clair 100 meters due east of John-Paul's and Balalaika's lakefront home.

God had thus helpfully enabled the wood-be suicide pilot to *drown* there and still achieve his goal of *dying*, but without killing his intended two targets. However, this literal *Act of God* had basically saved an empty *house*, since the suicide pilot's two targets had happened to be sleeping at their primary residence in Detroit overlooking the Detroit River that night.

John-Paul nonetheless gratefully thanked God for saving his lavish lakeside getaway, whereof he and his wife had grown quite fond since purchasing it at a comparatively bargain price the previous year.

The Imperial Coronation itself, while somewhat anticlimactic after all the events that had preceded it, nonetheless was a memorably majestic, solemn, and impressive affair, with invited heads of state from all over the globe in attendance.

The Imperially-appointed King Vladimir of Russia nevertheless declined to attend *despite* his appointment, so the Divine Eternal Presence unceremoniously *teleported* him to the affair and made the former Russian premier kneel before the newly-crowned King of America and Emperor of Earth, which caused John-Paul *enormous embarrassment*. Seeing Putin being forced to kneel, Kim Jong Un, the former "Supreme Leader" and now the Imperially-appointed King of North Korea, spontaneously went and knelt before John-Paul as well.

John-Paul would thereafter protest to the Presence in one of Their increasingly frequent sessions in the clouds, "Your Godliness, I don't want anyone *kneeling* before me *ever again*. That isn't the kind of *king* that I'm going to be, nor is it the *kingdom*—or indeed, the *empire*—that I personally envision.

"I also plan to conduct all of the business of ruling this American kingdom—and presently, the global empire—from my relatively less-than-imperial house on the lake and my even less imperial place on the river. There will be no royal or imperial palace for me. I leave the White House to Prime Minister Obama and the Capitol Building to the dukes and duchesses, marquesses and marchionesses, and barons and baronesses who formerly were United States Senators, Congresspersons, and U.S. Representatives.

"Soon I will need to decide which of them will permanently *keep* these titles and who among them will return to private life.

"Then I'm going to have to tackle the even more *trying* task of initiating and overseeing the establishment of my Resource-Driven and Technology-Driven Global Economic System—and I realize, too, that *this* may prove to be the hardest task of all."

All right, Your Imperial Majesty, the Presence said. *All of that is now* your *call—except for your commandeering of Roy Robber's* home *to turn it into a* museum. *He worked hard to get where he got against great odds, and I don't want you to take his house from him just because he* fired *you that time. Take away Trump Tower instead—and turn it into a museum with exhibits illustrating the history of the rise of absolute capitalism. I will help you as needed in all of your relevant undertakings—but as I said, I envision one of My primary functions here to be that of being your* Enforcer *when there are individuals or groups who unwisely refuse to go along with your egalitarian agenda for the planet.*

The Presence scratched Its beard.

Be aware that I incidentally have already reached down into the Macomb County Jail and stopped *the* hearts *of your two surviving would-be assassins who came across the lake from Canada in the boat. Former federal agents who now comprise your Imperial Guard will soon report that those men had flown into Canada from Colombia, using false identification papers.*

John-Paul frowned. "I'm a little sorry that Your Godliness saw fit to *smite* them. I had hoped to rehabilitate them and 'reboot' them as farmers. I intend to legalize the production and use of marijuana, and perhaps even some other drugs, and put the emphasis on *education* regarding substance abuse—including *alcohol*-abuse—to deal with those human failings."

Then boldly shaking his forefinger right in the Eternal Presence's *faux* Michelangelic Face, the old/new Emperor-Poet added, "If You *would*, in the future please let me *know* when You plan to kill someone, Your Almightiness, so I can perhaps at least have some *say* in the matter!"

I will, *whenever such counter-revolutionary groups and individuals have incidentally allowed me enough time to run the issue by you, Your Majesty—and you don't need to be shaking your puny little primate forefinger in My Face like that. I advise you not to do it again. We can talk more about some of these other things later.*

Now—*get yourself some* rest, *old man—because* believe *Me, in the weeks immediately to come in which you're going to bring your truly* revolutionary *RDTDES into play, you're really going to* need *that rest!*

XI.

Converting and then *accustoming* all potentially immortal human beings on Planet Earth to God's New World Order and the benevolent eternal rule of Earth's Emperor John-Paul III proved to occur much faster and more easily than the Emperor John-Paul and even God the Great Eternal Presence had imagined it would. John-Paul jetted alone in the converted and imperially-accoutered former American *Air Force One* to several African, Asian, South-American, and European countries to meet with their heads of state. Almost all of them expressed their eagerness to become faithful subjects of the New World Order which had been willed by God.

In Italy, the Emperor John-Paul was incidentally and particularly impressed by the beauty and charm of the youngest daughter of Federico Orsini, eighteenth Duke of Ferrara—the willowy Princess Paola—whom John-Paul met at a party on Capri in one of her father's several villas. He spent a considerable amount of (platonic) time with the pretty 22-year-old princess, which caused God the Great Eternal Presence to remark to him upon his early return to the seat of Imperial power in America,

I am extremely proud of you, Your Imperial Majesty. That gorgeous, aristocratic young girl was viscerally enamored of you and your lofty title, and for Your Majesty she would have been easy pickings*—but for perhaps the* first *of hundreds of times in your life, you desisted and resisted such temptation! Did you perhaps suspect that maybe I had planted her* *there to tempt you, as the fabled fallen angel Satan might have—and did you return to America early to avoid the temptation?*

"No, Your Godship—I sensed instinctively that You had not planted her in that manner. Given my advanced age and your relevant warning to me, resisting and desisting from such an indulgence was fairly easy. Besides, despite her age, the Earth-Empress Balalaika is *prettier* than the Princess Paola Orsini, and it has always been my intention, albeit belatedly, to remain faithful to my wife. I came home early because there are surprising pockets of resistance to the New World Order here in America that I need to deal with."

I had planned to alert you to those problems upon your return, John-Paul—to Me, of course, they had been no surprise whatever.

Surprisingly to John-Paul (but naturally not to God), most of the initial resistance to the New World Order was coming from the former *United States*—which like the British Empire, the sixteenth-century Holy Roman Empire, ancient Imperial Rome, Alexander of Macedon's great Greek Empire, and the ancient Persian, Assyrian, and Etruscan Empires before it—had become accustomed to occupying a lordly, bullying, wealth-driven, ethnocentric, and paternalistically *privileged* position on the planet.

Recently high-ranking politicians like Lord John Boehner, Michigan Grand Duke Rip Sniper, and disempowered corporate mogul Donald Trump had a particularly hard time adjusting to John-Paul's royal and imperial rule. After getting John-Paul's go-ahead, American Prime Minister Barack Obama had to replace Sniper as the Grand Duke of Michigan with Mark Schauer, former Republican governor Sniper's erstwhile Democratic rival for the Michigan governorship.

Also, following the Eternal Presence's earlier suggestion, John-Paul in his secondary role as the King of America had ordered American Prime Minister Obama to invoke the law of eminent domain upon Trump Tower and convert it to a museum containing artifacts and newsreels about capitalism. Thereupon, Donald Trump petitioned the Prime Minister to be granted the job of Curator of the museum.

Obama quickly granted that petition, and Mr. Trump set about gathering the artifacts.

In recognition of the emerging need for better-familiarizing Americans with their nation's history, the Prime Minister then issued a Ministerial Decree that all of the colleges and universities in the country were to add a course on Museum Curatorship to their curricula. As a result of Obama's historic Decree, similar but smaller museums would gradually pop up, open, and flourish all across America in the years to come.

Noting Obama's renewed attention to education, and having been a professional educator in the State of Michigan for most of his life, The Emperor John-Paul then set about helping Detroit and Michigan to become leaders again in the field of public education *overall*—kindergarten through graduate school.

He said to God,

"Your Divinity, in one of Our earlier conversations, I mentioned the fairy tale that the early nineteenth century Danish storyteller Hans Christian Anderson wrote about the naked emperor who was fooled by a shyster clothier into thinking that the nonexistent 'clothing' he had sold to him and that he had been dressed in by his man-servants was of fine ermine and velvet and was visible to all intelligent people, including the Emperor himself. It took an innocent child to blurt out the truth: '*But the Emperor has no clothes!*'

"In the persons of virtual 'emperors' who went by the titles of *governor*, *emergency manager* and *superintendent*, the Governor of Michigan and the Emergency Manager and the current Superintendent of the Detroit Public Schools have figuratively 'had no clothes.' To a lesser extent, that has also been the situation with emergency managers elsewhere in Michigan. The graduation rates in Detroit schools are far lower than officials announce—they're at an appalling 21 percent, and most of that 21 percent are girls.

"Following the 1999 state takeover of the Detroit Public Schools, the test scores of DPS students plummeted in a free fall to become the worst in the country. Less than half of Detroit's five-year-olds arrive at school ready to learn. Its fourth-graders are in the bottom ten percent in reading even compared with other large, impoverished cities, with an appalling 3 percent of Detroit kids rated as 'proficient.' Median reading levels in most of Detroit's public *high schools* are at the fourth-grade levels. Remedying this for Detroit for the rest of what once was disparagingly referred to as 'the Third World' is going to be one of my highest priorities as Emperor of Earth."

That's all well and good, John-Paul, God said. *And I commend you for your lifelong concern for bettering the education of* all *American children. However, there remain other and far more immediately pressing matters for Us to address;* ergo, *contrary to your Imperial decree that peace is now to reign unimpeded throughout the world, hostilities have still been occurring on the planet in several places. Be advised that I have had to take stern preventive action in that regard on your behalf.*

Indeed, what God told John-Paul about "hostilities still having been occurring" was an unfortunate and present problem that had had to be Divinely dealt with: Acting on orders from a few commanding officers on the field who had remained in stubbornly defiant insubordination to the Emperor of Earth, soldiers on both sides of the war in Afghanistan had fired upon each other, but the hot lead had stopped suddenly cold in midair and then had dropped to the ground, having been rendered harmless by an instantaneous Act of God.

Almost simultaneously, the same thing had miraculously happened between combatants in Libya, Syria, Israel/Palestine, Iraq, and the Ukraine.

It had also happened in Detroit and in some other American cities where drug dealers and teenaged gangs had continued to bear grudges and attempt to keep on killing each other.

It had had also happened in a minor skirmish on the North Korean/ South Korean border.

It also happened in Mexico and in Central and South America, where the Emperor John-Paul had rendered the previously enormously profitable and deadly drug trade instantly *profitless*, but where old grudges still illogically prevailed.

The Emperor John-Paul Jones III and American Prime Minister Barack Obama both personally addressed the United Nations General Assembly in New York City to reinforce and ensure compliance with John-Paul's Imperial Edict that all nations terminate all hostilities permanently. In his address, John-Paul promised that there would be no Holy "*smitings*" were the compliance to occur. Becoming aware of this promise and disagreeing with it, God came once again to the Emperor John-Paul and proclaimed,

Your Royal and Imperial Majesty, I must tell you that I have grown most impatient with this murderous insubordination to your global law. You asked Me to brief *you before I smote anyone. I am hereby* briefing *you: I have chosen to make a global example of those American generals and Taliban commanders in Afghanistan who disobediently refused to terminate hostilities. They will not see another sunrise on this Earth.*

Hearing this, the newly anointed Emperor became very upset. "Godliness, *please*—I promised the United Nations that You wouldn't *do* that. Also, for *God's sake*—er, I mean for the sake of *Your Divine justice* and for the sake of the wives and families of those errant U.S. officers, I don't want You to kill the *Americans*! Your Holy Godship has demonstrated already that all of the weapons on both sides are effective no longer and cannot take lives."

But these men intended *to take lives, John-Paul. They* tried *to take lives, in defiance of your law, which you have enacted in My Divine Name! How can I* not *smite them? They are equally* guilty *on both sides. I have no alternative other than to make an example of* all *of them.*

"Your Godliness, *here's* an alternative: Over the World-Wide Web, I'll send an Imperial Message to all national leaders and to all other citizens of the Empire of Earth, as well. This Imperial Message will state unequivocally that henceforth any individual who commits an act with murderous intent, or *commands* that such an act be committed—whether or not the act be *successful*—will thereby *die instantly* at Your Divine Hand. The Internet is indeed a marvelous tool: My Imperial Messages are now regularly reaching all seven billion souls, either directly or indirectly."

God deliberated for a moment and then said,

All right, John-Paul. Go ahead and send the message—but know that this *is going to be their* last chance.

XII.

The Emperor John-Paul lost no time sending the Message all across the Internet, and it had a most *salutary* effect on *99.9 percent* of the belligerents it targeted. Amazingly, following the Message, the Great Eternal Presence was obliged to smite only one terrorist commandant and two rogue American generals—both of them alcoholic egomaniacs who had lost total touch with reality and in truth could and probably *should* have been hospitalized in a rehabilitative or psychiatric ward. John-Paul genuinely mourned their deaths, and then in an Internet message to the United Nations representatives and the rest of the world, he formally expressed his deep regret at the three Divine smitings—but he also pointed out that the three transgressors had been duly warned.

John-Paul also mourned the guilty prisoners on the death rows across America when he learned that God had similarly dealt with *them* in terminal fashion.

He then announced to God, "Your Godliness, I am going to issue a worldwide edict to close all the jails and prisons and release all the prisoners. In the Empire of Earth, there is no longer any need for human incarceration of any kind."

In that case, said God, *I'm going to have to* stop *some of those released prisoners'* hearts from beating, *John-Paul. In prisons in some American states where capital punishment was illegal, there are evil men and women who won't fit into society and don't deserve immortality. I overlooked smiting them with the others who were incarcerated in American states where capital punishment is legal. It was a mere oversight on my part which I shall now correct.*

John-Paul put his palms and fingertips together in a gesture of prayer. "I'll *rehabilitate* these others whom you overlooked, Your Holiness—I *promise*! I have never been in favor of capital punishment. *Please*—I'm *praying* to You—don't smite them!"

What about the young Detroit drug dealer who shot the little two-year-old girl with a pistol at point-blank range because he wanted to punish her father? He took her life away long before she ever had a chance to live it.

John-Paul ruminated on that for only a few seconds and said, "All right—*him* You can go ahead and smite."

What about the man who shot the helpless homeless old men in cold blood?

"I guess You can smite him, too."

What about the men who cut off the beaks of live chickens and packed live pigs in crates without giving them room even to move and then shipped them off to be slaughtered?

"Your Godship can smite those evil m-----f------s [*four-syllable incest-implicative plural epithet*] too, for all I care! I used to be a member of PETA [*People for the Ethical Treatment of Animals*]."

I <u>know</u> *you were, John-Paul. Now you're starting to see it* My *way.*

So—what about the human traffickers in teenaged girls and the child molesters who are still out there running free, and the doddering old ex-Nazis in Paraguay and Bolivia and other parts of the world who escaped the Allied net in 1945? Also, what about some of Pol Pot's Khmer Rouge mass murderers and the remainder of the dictatorial Duvalier family's machete-wielding old Tonton Macoute *in Haiti who are still running loose? None of them deserve to be your immortal subjects in your Utopian Empire of Earth, do they?*

"No *way*—go ahead and smite every last one of those bastards!"

What about the Isis torturers and beheaders of the innocent?

"Ditto!"

What about misfit, miserable, smug, sick suburban teens who have plotted to shoot children in school?

"Well, I guess it's okay for You to put them out of their misery."

What about teenaged bullies—*both boys and girls?*

"No, not *them*—I'd rather try to *educate* them."

All right—then them I'll spare.

At that point, the Eternal Presence paused ominously and asked,

WHAT ABOUT GEORGE W. BUSH *? I am well aware of this poem you once wrote:*

'May Bush be shipped to Iraq
And get transfigured as a fly
Adrift above a dying rat
Beside a dead one, in July—
The rats to be fed to a hungry cat
That catches and eats the accursed fly
For the cat to excrete in the sweltering street

So the fly may emerge in the cat's oozing turd
That reeks and secretes in carnivorous heat
And then gets gobbled up by a turd-eater bird.'

And incidentally, whatever on Earth is a turd-eater bird*? I don't believe I ever* created *any such creature as a "turd-eater bird."* Vultures, *yes, and carrion-eating* crows*—but no "*turd-*eater birds."*

"You won't find the 'turd-eater bird' in any *ornithology book*, Your Godship, because the 'turd-eater bird' doesn't *exist*. However, had there *been* such a bird as the 'turd-eater bird,' the world could only have hoped that the turd-eater bird would have eaten George W. Bush before he had a chance to attack Iraq."

Well, this brings Me back to My question about Bush. And while I'm at it, what about CHENEY? I'm also well aware of another *poem you wrote entitled 'Bush & Cheney':*

'Those knaves need hoisting by their necks
Stretched past the points their necks will flex:
While oftentimes the odious
Can become malodorous,
The sounds of that pair
Kicking nothing but air
Perchance might prove
Melodious.'

Given the tone and tenor of those two poems of yours, do I therefore gather that now you will want me to smite *that pair of mendacious, mass-murderous traitors…?*

The Emperor John-Paul thought for a long moment before he answered God, in a flat tone of finality, "Your Almightiness, I reckon I'll leave those two villains to your tender mercies in that place where 'Mine eyes have seen the glory of the Coming of the Lord'—where You're 'stamping out the vintage where the Grapes of *Wrath* are stored'—at the moment when You 'loose the fateful lightning of Your terrible, swift *sword*.'"

Turning his attention then to more progressive and merciful matters, the old/new Emperor of Earth noted with immense satisfaction that his Resource-Driven and Technology Driven Economic System (RDTDES) was taking hold *worldwide* far sooner and more readily than he had thought it would. Every able human subject of the Emperor was doing some sort of job for which each was best-qualified, and some were performing *multiple* ones, bartering their valuable services to their fellow humans, who returned alternative services to them *in kind*, when able.

The one minor and temporary problem that did crop up in every country in this regard was the reluctance of too many citizens to dig ditches, clean streets, clean toilets, haul garbage, repair broken sewer mains, and perform other menial and sometimes hard and messy tasks. The Emperor's designated national leaders solved this problem in various ways that were benevolent and fair. The most frequent two solutions were lotteries and a citizen draft.

After the Empire of Earth had been established in his 85 percent black hometown of Detroit and in black communities across America, the Emperor John-Paul in his dual capacity as America's king was gratified to note that the black-on-black violence had virtually ceased. This was the "invisible" violence that hadn't often been reported, but it had targeted the community fiercely on many fronts, including the *miseducation* where the neighborhood school was unavailable or abandoned or neglected, and the available charter school was mismanaged and fixated on standardized tests. This was the "invisible" violence that had come at the urban society from chronic and massive unemployment, and it was the "invisible" violence against young people and seniors who had found recreation centers closed and parks overgrown—and who had to maneuver a bullet-proof partition to buy a quart of milk they hoped wasn't out-of-date after walking past blocks of devastating blight that surrounded them. Prior to the onset of the Empire, government policy had created the blight, the abandonment, and much of the violence in the black communities throughout America. The country had slashed the social safety net, draining the cities to fund the military in battles around the planet in the name of a democracy that had degenerated into a corporatocracy. Prior to the onset of the Empire of Earth, the violence in black cities in Michigan had been massaged and refined into the public policy called "emergency management." Black citizens had been stripped of their democracy which John-Paul had managed to restore in another way, although "democracy" wasn't what he or the Eternal Presence called it anymore.

Up in the sky with the Presence again, the live but temporarily disembodied spirit of the Emperor John-Paul again stretched out in his phantom chair and put his feet up on his phantom footstool—and this time both John-Paul and the Presence enjoyed a celebratory glass or two of Grand Marnier.

John-Paul, The Eternal Presence said, as It also stretched out and relaxed in Its own phantom chair and sipped Its drink, *I never told you about one of your poems that really* got *to me a long time ago. After I read it, I knew even way back then that one day I would be tapping you to do this job.*

"Which poem was *that,* Your Godship?"

It was a sonnet *that you wrote* twenty-seven years *ago—'Sonnet for a Safer Sea.'*

"Oh, yes—I remember it well. In fact, it's one of my few poems that I have actually committed to memory:

'This voyage of historic *humankind*
Is one whereon we're fated to decide
If cold creations of the corporate mind
Shall specify the way we'll live, or die.

We cruise now with mere *nautical* controls
Which navigate us up no harbor path:
We try to steer through antisocial shoals
With *sextants*, when we need a *sociograph*.
We automate our elemental selves—
Computerized, transistorized, yet *blind*...
And thus meander toward unfathomed hells
Whence it will prove impossible to find
The sort of *social* innovations we
Must seek, to sail upon a *safer* sea.'

Yes—that's *the one. You know, John-Paul, I always wanted a* poet *to head up the New World Order—this new* Empire of Earth—*because poets not only* feel *more* sensitively *than most other folk do, and they have more progressive societal insights than others do, but they can also put those feelings into words that affect others* deeply *enough to galvanize them into humanitarian action.*

Also, I was hopeful that under a poet's leadership *and a poet's* government, *poetry, philosophy, and the other humane arts would get the Imperial level of attention they deserve and would therefore* flourish—*as they did in ancient Greece, as they did in Elizabethan England and in the Italian city-states during the High Renaissance, and as they did in France during the bravest and brightest days of the Enlightenment and later during the days of Rodin, Lautrec, Matisse, Cezanne, and Dali. I truly believe that your Resource-Driven and Technology-Driven Economic System will be a catalytic force in causing this to happen.*

As God had hoped, in *Detroit* and even in *Warren, Michigan* and *Cleveland, Ohio*—as well as everywhere else in the United States of America and all throughout the Empire of Earth—the Emperor John Paul's RDTDES did indeed enable the humane arts to begin to flourish like they hadn't anywhere on the planet within previous *centuries*. Nothing so creatively *glorious* as this had happened since the Enlightenment had dawned in France or since the arts had flourished on the Italian peninsula during the days of the High Renaissance—

or even since the days of the great playwright Plautus and the philosopher Plato and the anonymous sculptor of the 'Winged Victory of Samothrace' in ancient Greece.

Both the Emperor of Earth and the Divine Eternal Presence also saw the Liberal Arts in this new Earth-age as now representing the foremost academic division in the field of *higher education*. They saw the Humanities as occupying a resurfaced '*Atlantis*' whose geniuses had once been driven out of their jobs and even out of their *countries* by unfriendly pedagogical and governmental regimes. Now they would no longer have to languish as refugees in limbo but could come out into the sun and shine again.

John-Paul took particular pride in the artistic renaissance that was emerging practically in *his own backyard*. In Dearborn, Michigan, Collette Cullen produced her play about the life of the deaf and blind Helen Keller's teacher Annie Sullivan, *Annie Speaks*, to critical acclaim and presently brought it to Broadway. Detroit-area social essayists Mitch Albom, Thomas Stephens, Curt Guyette, Stephen Henderson, Jack Lessenberry, Russ Bellant, and Dr. Sharon Howell became read popularly *world-wide*.

A Michigan graphic artist named Tom Stanton who never had been able to sell many of his beautifully rendered and fancifully psychedelic ink drawings became lionized state-wide for his talent. He then set up a brisk bartering business for his intricate creations, many of which he put on Facebook. An African-American painter from Detroit named Angelo Sherman who went simply by the name "Angelo," Royal Oak, Michigan sculptor Robert Landry, and Detroit autobiographer Yusef Shakur did the same.

Clinton Township, Michigan poet Donald Frederickson also did the same with his historic poetic sagas of the Vikings, with similar success. Prof. Rhoda Stamell did the same with her book of short narratives *Detroit Stories* and her novel *The Art of Ruin*. Songwriter and guitarist Thomas William Kozma did the same with his cleverly rhyming tunes. American poets M. L. Liebler, Melba Joyce Boyd, Jim Perkinson, Sherina Sharpe, Alford G. Harris, Khadijah Shabazz, Matthew Schatmeyer, Aurora Harris, Anthony Stachurski, Satori Shakoor, Mildred Williams and Wardell Montgomery of the Detroit Unity Poets, and Natasha "Beautiful Thought" Ane'e became internationally celebrated nearly overnight and read their poems in gatherings all throughout the Empire.

So did a certain octogenarian poet named John-Paul Jones the Third, the Empire's already famous (or in some few recently still-resentful circles *infamous*) Emperor. Old Poet John-Paul the *Prolific* was all too eager to share some of his favorite poems *repeatedly*, including the following cosmic one, which had been one of the *Infinite and Foreverlasting PRESENCE* 's favorites as *well*:

Yesterday Is Tomorrow

The cosmos bides its un-beginning end.
If *Bear* could see or *Crab* could comprehend,
This microcosmic rebel might be seen
Upon one shining pebble gleaming green.
Our end is our beginning's nether twin.
Within this measured stint, *shall be* has been
And never evermore again can be.
I fancy yet I could have met, *resigned*,
That pre-chaotic canceling of mind—
Foreverlasting darkness un-designed—
Had here but been no existential *she*.

That poem had appeared many years earlier in the *Sharon* (Connecticut) *Creative Arts Foundation Journal*. The "she" in the poem John-Paul did not name, but she had been the most significantly sparkling and *sparking* flame of his youth. Particularly gratifying to all who read or heard those eleven rhyming lines of iambic pentameter was the miraculous fact that God had now nullified the fearsome prospect of "foreverlasting darkness" for them *forever*.

Even *mentally challenged* world citizens contributed their talents to the new Empire of Earth. One example of this was a young autistic black man named Michael in Brooklyn, New York whose mother had bought him a cheap electronic piano keyboard in pre-Empire times when currency still had extrinsic value. The young man began to compose complex concertos in the classical style and play them on it, ultimately performing on gleaming grand pianos over network television and before audiences in concert halls all across America.

Michael also obtained a computer, got on the Internet, and began to study the *theory* of music. Amazingly, he then mastered the intellectual complexities of *appoggiatura* and *acciaccatura* and started teaching musical theory to children and interested adults in the little spare time he now had.

In doing this, he quickly learned to converse less haltingly and more logically. Having always been instantaneously able to compute the answers to complex mathematical problems, he then began to study advanced mathematics beyond Calculus and devised an entirely new (post-Einsteinian) mathematical model for ascertaining relative distances in intergalactic space, the fourth dimension.

Almost at the same time, another autistic world citizen—a nonetheless classically educated teenaged girl in Honduras—wrote some incredible transcendental poetry in pure Castilian Spanish which more than a thousand literature buffs translated into their various tongues and put on the Internet.

Simultaneously, yet a *third* autistic world citizen—a very, very old woman in Taiwan—devised a workable model for creating automobile and aircraft fuel from the abundant hydrogen in the world's oceans.

Her work thus was visceral to helping the Emperor achieve one of the Empire's paramount goals—the re-greening and greening-over of the entire planet through the replacement of the destructive fossil fuels that had been generating global warming and savaging the ozone.

The fabulous successes of the young autistic man, the old autistic woman, and the teenaged autistic girl inspired the Emperor John-Paul to petition the Divine Eternal Presence to cure all congenitally mentally and *physically* challenged human beings who were to remain extant on the planet—which petition He/It graciously granted.

On the occasion of Its/His granting this petition, the Eternal Presence reflected magnanimously,

I should have thought of doing that Myself, Your Imperial Majesty. Keep up the good work.

I do *have two suggestions, though. My first suggestion involves the LARGE HEDRON COLLIDER—that new particle-accelerator in Switzerland. Last fall, its operators put it into experimental "collision mode," and two proton beams were sent rocketing through a gargantuan underground tunnel in opposite directions and caused hundreds of millions of head-on crashes every second—each generating an infinitesimal fireball that briefly reproduced conditions not extant since a millionth of a millionth of a second after the cataclysm I caused that I like to call the Beginning of Worlds.*

If they conduct such an experiment again, the Collider could even produce revelations *(non-Biblical) regarding the existence of* multi-dimensional space—infinite *dimensions that are* independent of My creation *which may exist beyond the fourth dimension, and phenomena which even* I—*your Dauntless* Deity—*am reluctantly admitting only to Your Majesty that I am yet unable to fathom fully yet and am therefore continuing to contemplate without revealing the nature and outcomes of those contemplations to any living creature in my universe—not even* you. *Were its operators to botch the process even* slightly *when they put the LARGE HEDRON COLLIDER into 'collision mode" (an* unsettling *term) this coming autumn again, it could tilt your planet on its axis or even knock it out of its orbit around your sun—or even send it spinning into another* dimension beyond even My *control.*

So my first suggestion is that you stop them from *performing this potentially dangerous experiment.*

"Godliness, I *will* stop them from performing it."

That's good, because it could also send your planet plummeting in cold darkness toward one of those fearsome and inescapable black holes *out there, which embody one of My* own *botched experiments. I have boasted to you that I am Perfection* personified *and am often anthropomorphized as such in song and story, myth and fable, throughout the vast reaches of the universe that* are within my control, *but—and I will only ever tell* you *this, O My chosen Emperor John Paul, and I ask you to guard this secret—truly, I am not* entire *and* total Perfection, *and there are significant portions of the cosmos that I do* not *control! Those forbidden and* forbidding *outer regions aren't being controlled at* all, *by* anything.

Earlier, you told me a joke that contained a message. *Now let me tell* you *this story that contains a* moral.

Here is the story—

A Sagacious Old Man on a Mountaintop once shared this Sagacious Secret with a selected circle of his young disciples:

"Life *is a* fountain.*"*

After a moment of reflection on this profound bit of wisdom that the Sagacious Old Man on the Mountaintop had shared with him and his fellow disciples, one of the Sagacious Old Man's young disciples asked him,

"O Sagacious Old Man on the Mountaintop, would you be good enough to kindly explain to us the rare and lofty rationale that supports this Sacred Secret that you have shared with us?"

The Sagacious Old Man on the Mountaintop tugged at a white beard very similar to yours and Mine and scratched his head in thought for a long while. Finally, he said,

"You mean life ISN'T *a fountain?"*

The moral of that story, John-Paul, is that you should seek out no Sacred and Sagacious Seer such as even Myself *to find answers to your questions regarding how to advance your new Empire of Earth. Rather, for most of those questions, I exhort you to seek* within yourself *for the answers, because the Kingdom of God is indeed* within *you.*

I chose you for this endless and awesome task because you have been a lifelong, humane, and sensitive poet *first and foremost—and a true and honest poet can conceptualize and* create *a universe nearly as well as a* god *can. While* I*—your All-Seeing, All-Knowing and most Divine Deity—know whenever even a tiny* sparrow *falls,* you too *are* sensitive *and* sympathetic *to even that* fallen sparrow, *which I know that you then* mourn *in your merciful heart of hearts…and were it but for* that reason alone, *you have already amply demonstrated to Me that you were My best and most benevolent choice to rule this new and benevolently egalitarian empire.*

"I am humbled by Your Godship's confidence in me. I promise You that I will be worthy of your trust."

I know *you will, John-Paul.*

My second *suggestion to you is* this*: It would absolutely* delight *me if you would see fit to evict some of the remaining assorted kings, sheiks, princes, and former bank presidents and other nefarious corporate hon-*

chos throughout the world from their huge, ornate, and multitudinous palaces and turn those edifices into community centers or theme museums.

"That is something that I had already *planned* to do, Your Godship—now I'll tend to it immediately."

And the Emperor John-Paul *did* tend to it forthwith—after which the enormously pleased and more and *more* impressed Divine Eternal Presence intoned sonorously from on high,

Great job, John-Paul, great job! I'm gratified to see that you're well on your way to engendering the kind of egalitarian and benign empire that features everything you and I envisioned together when I first spoke to you back in your Earth month of July, which now seems even to Me *to be such a long time ago.*

"Thanks again, Your Godship. And yes—many wonderful and miraculous things have happened on Earth since then. Now I have two suggestions for *You*, too."

What are your two suggestions, *John-Paul?*

"Well, they're more in the form of two *requests*. Here is my first request:

The Ebola virus has the potential to become a pandemic all throughout the Empire of Earth, and there exist forms of cancer and other diseases that once would have been fatal to humans, but no longer *are* fatal because my subjects now have attained *immortality* via Your Divine Hand. Since now they can no longer *die* from these diseases but still can *contract* them, this will cause them to suffer *chronically*. Would you therefore please to eliminate these viruses and other diseases from the planet?"

Yes, John-Paul—I can do that. What is your second request?

O Mighty One, last winter I cracked two vertebrae in my back, and my back still hurts from it, along with my nagging old arthritis pain caused by the brutal athletic competitions of my youth."

All right, John-Paul—That is not a problem. I will make the pain go away.

"No—it's *more* than that, Your Godship—and it's not just for *me.* When my subjects have a toothache or backache or some other kind of piercing pain that tells them they need medical treatment, rather than have them *feel* that pain, couldn't you maybe just *ring a bell in their ears* to alert them that they need to seek treatment? That way, they won't have to *suffer.*"

That's an intriguing idea, John-Paul. However, it is a far more anatomically complicated *request than you realize. I will have to work on it.*

Now let me share one last thought with you before I go off for a while to a faraway galaxy to set some of those repeatedly wayward Klingons straight *again:*

I am pleased that in addition to being an artist and a poet, you are also an occasional violinist. *Well, one of your favorite fellow poets—the late Englishman T. S. Eliot— once wrote a cosmically paradoxical poem titled 'Burnt Norton' that used the* violin *as a* metaphor. *I now quote from that poem:*

Not the stillness of the *violin,* while the *note* lasts—
Not *that,* only—but the *coexistence…*
Or say that the *end precedes* the *beginning*
And the *end* and the *beginning* were always there
Before the *beginning* and after the *end.*

And you, *John-Paul—once when you hopefully, convolutedly, and* paradoxically *contemplated the* possible impossibility *of an* end *to* endlessness, *you coincidentally poeticized:*

Time = Infinity.

Eternally and yearningly,
mutual human multitudes
pray and chant
and chant and pray
in churches, temples, or mosques;
on their knees
(or on their faces pressed to prayer rugs);
They pray and chant and chant and pray
To a theoretical and longed-for
Eternal Presence (or Presences):

World WITHOUT END, amen, *amen.*

'Our end is our beginning's nether twin.
Within this measured stint, *shall be* has been
And never evermore again can be…'

And then you concluded *it,*

(but then again, *who really knows?—*

Perhaps it *can*!)

So now, *John-Paul,* I*—your Most Holy and Divine* Deity*—have made known unto you, and again I* say *unto you, and* through you *unto all of the living, breathing, teeming humanity down there, that it* can *indeed:*

That which has been shall be again *for all Eternity!*

The prospect of endless darkness will itself *one day* also *come to an end* forever *for all of the peace-loving faithful who have gone before you and have once dwelt* righteously *upon your Earth.*

Remember, too, that the Kingdom of Heaven dwells within *you. It dwells* within *you, remember!*

John-Paul Jones the Third, there once was a time when you and I were about to part for a while that I said unto you, "I would bid you now to go with God, were it not for the fact that I Myself am *God—and I am with you* already."

Know ye now that I am in the skies with sparrows and in the rustling of the leaves of summer and in the rush of rivers and the sweep of oceans.

Know that I am in in the lowly rat warrens and the rabbit burrows and with a shabbily dressed old black woman with a cane and swollen ankles standing in a crowded bus in Biloxi in your Earth month of August, and I am with the formerly frightened soldiers who were on both sides of conflicts and conflagrations past who wanted only to return to their families alive—and now they have!

Know that I am everywhere in every place; and know ye *also this day*

that I am with you always—

even unto the end of the EARTH.

An Evolutionary Epilogue

Dear Reader, do *NOT—repeat—*do *NOT*—put this book *down* just yet!!!

In all *fairness* (and in somewhat *guilty conscience*), your devious old author needs to tell you that it would be *most intellectually dangerous* for you to *do* that!

I'll say it once *again*: Don't close this book *without reading this significantly lengthy but* *<u>necessary</u>* *Epilogue....*

Let us reflect for a moment upon the book's *Prologue* scene at the hospital way back on page 13 when the activist educator poet John-Paul Jones the Third first awakened with a *steel plate in his head* from the long coma into which he had fallen following his automobile accident.

At this present point in your reading, Dear Reader, it is to be presumed (and also fervently *hoped*) that you are *sitting down.*

If you're *not* sitting down, it is highly advisable that you *do sit down at once* and take a very *deep* breath. The reason that it is so highly advisable for you to do this is because it now must be solemnly and regretfully *revealed* to you here that it was at John-Paul's memorable (and actually *truly* miraculous) *awakening moment* from his *coma* (as recounted in the *Prologue* to this little book) that the old octogenarian poet first came to realize with a feeling of deep *dismay* that *everything* he had "experienced" during the two months when he lay in that coma with a *metal plate* in his head and a *stent* sewn onto his aortal artery, slowly recovering from the car crash, had all been but an

ELABORATE,

HOPELESSLY IMPOSSIBLE,

UTOPIAN

DREAM

that he had *dreamt* while balancing back and forth on the teeter-totter of the two extremities between *living* or *dying.*

This stark and stunning realization recalled to his mind a derivative *poem* of only two lines that he had penned nearly *seventy years earlier* as an unusually *reflective* child poet:

Might everything we see or seem
Be but a *dream within* a *dream*?

He now sinkingly sensed that the *Great Eternal Presence* had *never* spoken to him.

He would never *be* the immortal Poet-*Emperor of Earth.*

Men's reason was *still* deformed and their souls were *still* in malaise—and now neither their *bodies nor* their souls would evidently be *saved.* The wars and killing and pervasive bigotry and corruption and exploitation and injustice would continue to occur in Detroit and Michigan and everywhere else all across the face of our battered old planet.

His lovely wife Balalaika would never be an *Empress Eternal*, and his family and friends would never receive royal and noble titles and become immortal. The only "earth" that he and they would ever need *eternally* would be *six feet of it* beneath which to be buried.

Close to tears, old John-Paul the Poet asked a kind and accommodating young nurse to fetch him a pen. When she brought it, he slowly jotted down this simple quatrain:

<u>I</u> – <u>tinerant</u>

All I am, or can be now,
Or remain content to be,
Is an itinerant old prow
Parting a poetic sea.

He considered the *immensity* of his <u>own</u> *sea*—the 23-mile-wide Lake St. Clair overlooking his imposing house under the often majestically mountainous white-and-purple clouds wherein he had dreamed that he had sat with the Eternal Deity formulating Their plan for the benign and benevolent Empire of Earth. He ruefully reflected upon the character Ishmael's melancholy query about the ocean's vast and forbidding whiteness in Herman Melville's prodigious novel *Moby Dick* that he had first read in his teens:

"Is it that by its *indefiniteness* it shadows forth the heartless voids and immensities of the universe, and thus stabs us from behind with the thought of *annihilation*, when beholding the white depths of the Milky Way?"

Then, growing even more deeply despondent, he penned these five terse lines:

<u>20—?</u>

In death I’ll lie in endless gloom
With “Poet” carved upon my tomb,
And life’s long quilt run through the loom.
Time past was *pawn*, and *place* mere *space*:
At last I’m gone without a trace....

BUT *THEN—*

Suddenly, in the midst of his contemplation of his poetically phrased “pre-chaotic canceling of *mind*” and of the impending oblivion whereof he had poignantly poeticized in his poem ‘Yesterday Is Tomorrow,’ the heartbroken old poet almost fancied that very *faintly* he could hear a protesting and somehow quite familiar and plainly *present* ‘*Presence*’ calling to him from somewhere deep inside his still-yearning mind:

O John-Paul, ye of little faith! Did I not say unto you that you must seek within yourself *to find the Answers—for the Kingdom of God is* within you*? Did I not* tell *you that, John-Paul?*

The intrusive ‘Voice’ seemed to become louder, *stronger*:

And did I not say unto you, ‘I am with you always, *even unto the END OF THE* EARTH*??’*

Wanting to believe in spite of himself that he had actually *heard* that familiar, Divine Voice uttering those wonderful words to him once again, John-Paul sat up straight in bed. Scarcely daring to answer the *seemingly returned* phantom Presence, he began with steadily mounting excitement to write again furiously and feverishly, this time writing for *God*, *to* God, and writing this time with God deep *within* him:

<u>Leaves of Ice</u>

(in partial tribute to Walt Whitman)

Following a freezing rain
On a sun-bright winter morn,
I was born a bawling bairn
In my snow-topped Motown home.

Leaves of ice popped up by chance
And shone on drooping bits of branch.
Sparkling from stark silhouette,
They glitter in the winter yet.

With some minor mixed supports
Through the dastard decades since,
I've fought folks with frozen hearts
And hardened heads and minds of mince.

(Some I've loved and some I've not—
The unloved ones I've left to rot.)

Today I wish at last to see
Those sparkly, star-tipped branches free
From greedy grip of icy bead
And then in shortened order sprout
New green-grown leaves from free-born seed
Perhaps yet one more time, *flat-out*!

NOW you're <u>COOKING</u>, *O John-Paul the Poet,* THE DIVINE AND ETERNAL PRESENCE exclaimed to him—for indeed it *was* truly He. *That's more* <u>like</u> *it!*

Thus so <u>*Divinely*</u> encouraged, the hopeful old activist versifier still didn't quite dare to answer or even quite dare to *believe*. Instead, he wrote ever more feverishly, his pen literally *racing* now across the page:

In the *Interim*: Intimation of *Immortality*

(in partial tribute to William Wordsworth and T. S. Eliot)

I've raced *interim* sprinters in *interim* races,
Loved *interim* women in *interim* places,
Been *interim* chief of Detroit's troubled schools
(And of *Madison's* briefly, contending with fools).
Between the desire and the base spasm
Whence once we were sired to cross the great chasm,
From that fast *coming*
Until the last *going*,
Between our first stirring
And final interring,
Indeed, we're *all* *interim*—

(Yet just *in* the *INTERIM*...????)

All right, My aged and esteemed poet, the old, familiar Eternal Presence declared to him—*I can plainly see what you have just pointedly* poeticized *so questioningly, and I fully empathize with your needful longing to* know.

The True Living God now hesitated for a moment only—but to John-Paul that moment seemed an Eternity.

Then God continued emphatically, *I am now going to entrust you with My* ANSWER *to that all-encompassingly* cosmic *question which you so yearningly posed in the last line of that poem.*

Are you ready to hear *it?*

Putting his pen aside, John-Paul was finally yet still very *tentatively* able to attempt to answer the returned Presence.

"I'm all *ears*, Your Divine Godliness," he managed to whisper.

What did you say, *John-Paul? I couldn't* hear *you.*

"I'm all *ears*," John-Paul said in a slightly louder voice. Then he added in a soft murmur, "And I'm so *relieved* to be privileged to experience Your Holy Voice again."

What *did you say, John-Paul? I* still *couldn't* hear *you.*

Sucking in a very deep breath, John-Paul lifted his voice then and verily *shouted*, "I *hear You*, Your Great and Everlasting Lordness! I'm all *ears*! I'm all *EARS*!!"

Good! Here, then, for your EARS *to* hear, *and for your yearning* HEART *to* internalize, *is My Divine ANSWER to that* cosmic question *which you have just posed to Me, John-Paul:*

As I have intimated to you already, you and all of your righteous *kind will sit enthroned beside Me in Heaven on one glorious day of judgment.*

Meanwhile, *in that long* INTERIM *whereof you have written in that* rhyme, *you must continue to do My Work down there on* Earth. *You must do this not in some oligarchic* empire *or* quasi-*empire or* would-be *empire that We had misguidedly devised together in that dream wherein I appeared unto you, but rather in your* own *desperately* embattled DEMOCRACY, *which despite its many flaws remains the noblest form of government ever devised by the mind of man, and one which you and your righteous fellows must fight to defend* democratically*—and defend with your very* lives, *if necessary—both* beyond *and* within *the borders of your great nation.*

And on that *count—on that generically* GLOBAL question *of whether or not* **DEMOCRACY** *is the* best *and indeed the* only righteous form of human government—*My* Divine Godliness *is sheepishly obliged to have to admit that this Ordinarily* Almighty *and* Omnipotent Godhead *whom you once dreamed was hovering Holily up in some fluffy cumulous cloud and sporting a white, anthropomorphically Michelangelan beard*

was **WRONG**

and YOU *were* **RIGHT**

all along!

Unwittingly, your admittedly and shamefacedly errant *Deity played a cruel cosmic joke on you in that dream—and* in *it, My* low *opinion of democracy indeed was an* erroneous *one which I now* retract.

So, *John-Paul—although it's regrettably true that you cannot ever be the benign and benevolent* Poet-*Emperor of EARTH whereof I deceptively enabled you to fantasize in that long and impossibly Utopian dream, it remains My rare (and apologetic) pleasure to make amends to you today by* anointing *you* as *and* appointing *you to* be "Emperor" *of the* Earth's POETS!

It is My sincere hope that you will look upon this retributive poetic Anointment *and* Appointment, *if you will, as a kind of Divine* **Consolation Prize**.

At this point, the now-beatified poet John-Paul felt the hairs on the back of his neck stand up: He felt a transforming, all-enveloping warmth, and he experienced a deep and genuine epiphany.

"Then, Almighty Godhead," this newly and duly *anointed* and *appointed* old octogenarian 'Emperor' of the Earth's *Poets* proclaimed, "my poetic *heart* will continue to *burn to defend democracy* until this poetically pulsing, fist-sized fiber of militant muscle and blood bursts beneath my breastbone! In Your Holy Name, and for as long as I live, I will write poems, essays, and perhaps even more *books* offering revolutionary/*evolutionary* solutions to problems such as war and global warming and bigotry and religious intolerance and illiteracy and the drug trade and corporate greed—all those soul-destroying evils that confront the spread of world democracy.

"In my writings and addresses—in the spirit of cautioning our future leaders never to repeat the mistakes of their predecessors—I will *elucidate* our nation's errant leadership during the administration of our 43rd President, who arrogantly and shortsightedly believed that what is best for America is always best for the entire Earth. For example, his policy in the Middle East was based upon what he called "American Internationalism"—which was about an ongoing U.S. *imperialism* and retaining control of natural resources, about carving up continents like pieces of meat, and about installing imperialistically complicit and compliant dictators and moving them around like chess pieces and then violently removing them when they no longer served his imperialist purpose. Thus, it also was about leaving the indigenous peoples with scraps and pottage.

"Over a quarter-century ago, I authored a planning booklet published by the Rochester Community Schools' Division of Instruction when I was the Deputy Superintendent there. In it, Your Godship will recall that I wrote,

"'Beyond educators' instructing for career success alone, there also exists a classical set of timeless teachings that our children should learn for those teachings' own sake alone. Our youth must come to understand how Western civilization evolved from the Sumerian to the modern, and to know that ancient and rich human histories exist that are Far Eastern and African rather than only *Western*, and to understand how Plato informs the process of Knowing, and to know how Nietzsche's nihilism and Machiavelli's cynical wisdom inform the history of politics, and how Ghandi's paradigm of passive resistance freed India and offered Dr. King a strategic model for the American civil rights movement—and how the Renaissance priest Martin Luther's doctrine of free will transformed the Western World.'"

Jean-Paul paused for breath and continued, with mounting and near-orgasmic intensity:

"*Domestically*, I will begin by making *ten proposals* to the United States Congress, which, by the way, I *prosaically prophesy* will become overwhelmingly, benightedly, (and potentially *tragically*) *Republican* after the midterm elections in November, 2014 in a partially (and *covertly*) ongoing racist reaction to the 2008 ascendance and 2012 reelection of African-American Barack Obama to the Presidency:

"My *first* proposal is that a *graduated income tax* be enacted nationwide with significant portions of it to be applied to K-12 and higher education, including to K-12 charters and other non-traditional schools (on the condition that they be genuinely measured by the same standards and held accountable to the same level of governance as the traditional schools);

"my *second*, that a constitutional referendum be held to establish more balanced *population representation* in the Senate and House: for example, it is an anachronistic absurdity that hugely populated California and tiny Rhode Island each have *two senators*;

"the *third*, that political campaign contributions be strictly regulated and publicly reported;

"the *fourth*, that Congressional legislation be enacted establishing a minimum wage of $15 per hour with annual cost-of-living adjustments;

"the *fifth*, that legislation be enacted demanding an end to business secrets and swindles—and that this legislation require expert and unbiased public examination of the books of banks and corporations before they are permitted to seek concessions from employees or garner governmental tax breaks;

"the *sixth*, that the adult use of intoxicative drugs be decriminalized and pertinent counter-education be increased;

"the *seventh*, that the debilitating student loans be forgiven;

"the *eighth*, that the Congress foster the feminists' fair movement for equal pay for equal work;

"the *ninth*, that neo-Rooseveltian legislation be enacted that provides for a) the opportunity for full employment *nationwide*, b) governmental subsidization of poets, artists, classical musicians, and educationally and scientifically innovative thinkers, c) permanent public-works *environmental restoration programs* with *genuine* community input and expert infrastructure-analysis to be performed *regularly, d)* strengthened legislation that protects the physical, educational, and emotional rights of children with special needs, and *e)* the 'green revolution' to be brought to the forefront in an endeavor to reverse global warming worldwide.

"Regarding Number Nine," John-Paul added, "I believe that there is still time for us to avoid catastrophic warming, but not within the rules of capitalism as they are currently constructed."

He then concluded, "My *tenth* proposal to the Congress is that it finally mount overdue, genuine, determined, and *fruitful* efforts to enforce the Supreme Court's 1954 Brown vs. Board of Education ruling to integrate schools racially, and that it earnestly endeavor to likewise integrate residential communities all throughout the land as well. Also, that it cooperate in patriotically *bipartisan* fashion in *this* and in *all nine* of my *other* proposals, while simultaneously maintaining a robust military for the defense of our precious democracy and of the human rights of *all* its citizens.

"O God of all the ages, in my poems I promise to sing songs of a shining democratic city that develops progressive practices embodying the contours of a new, compassionate, and sustainable urban life—of a shining city steeped in the African-American, Latino, and Celtic traditions of *freedom-fighting*, of progressive *labor-organizing*, and of *artistic visioning*—and thus of a shining democratic city emerging from industrial devastation as a *new and nurturing kind of metropolis*.

"In Detroit, we already are actively re-imaging urban life on principles of *sustainability*, *cooperation*, *productivity*, and *joy*: We are creating new forms of work and a more life-affirming *culture*. We are also becoming known as a grass-roots global leader in *urban agriculture*. We are developing and *re*-developing new/*old* methods of local food production for *local consumption*. Also, we already have small but growing craft, graphic art, spoken-word, and other forms of *purely local* offerings—with endeavors toward *sustainability*, *social responsibility*, *racial integration*, and *self-determination*. We are initiating forms of *place-based* education that engage young people as "solutionaries"—learning, and in turn *teaching*—as they join hands to build and restore community. All across the city, we are contracting for community-owned and operated *low-power* (LP) FM radio stations, *e.g.*, WNUC LP/FM 96.7 Detroit (NorthEndWoodward.org) that will tell true and contemporary tales of big-corporation exploitations of grassroots citizens which the corporate-collusive major local media shrink from telling.

"Our venerable old Motor City is evolving within this revolutionary vision that challenges the soulless *corporate* view of urban centers and their people. Ours is a liberating vision that celebrates cities as places for *all* people to develop and thrive in *just* and *caring* ways. This bright, new, purely *democratic* Motown vision has the potential to shake the very foundation of an oligarchic corporate America whose tentacles presently threaten to envelop and enthrall the entire Earth. So in *all* of those regards, as Your anointed new "Emperor of *Poets*" and also as a *belated* and no longer *reluctant believer* in Your *Divinity*, I offer up to You this devotional poetic couplet:

"Ascent to *Heaven* in the Subjective Case

"A poet *heart* will burn as coal
'Til it *surrender* up its *soul*."

Having recited this spontaneous and impassioned little verse to the Divine Eternal Presence and outlined to Him/It these ten egalitarian proposals for America's legislators—and having also described to Him/It his hopeful model for his ideal conceptual community—John-Paul the Poet felt what he later could only describe to Balalaika as an all-enveloping sensation of *beatific calm.*

It had also been at that same memorably poetic recitative moment that John-Paul Jones the Third—now for the first time feeling about his shoulders the fresh folds of the purple mantle of the Divinely anointed and appointed *Emperor of the Earth's Poets*—knew for sure that for the precious few flesh-and-blood *Earth*-years remaining to him, his egalitarian *poetry-to-come* would therefore have thrillingly soulful and *Holy inspiration.* He also thrilled to the ultimate and unequivocal realization that the Infinite Godly *Goodness* of the Holy Spirit would truly be *with* him and *within* him *always...*

,,,even unto the end of the *EARTH.*

Appendix 'A'

For discerning fans of *protest poetry*, as "The Great Eternal Presence" professed Himself/Itself to be in this allegorical book, and as are many of you social-activist readers out there with a bent for verse, your old activist author-poet is including the following four localized poems as "out-takes" in this book similar to those out-takes at the ends of movies that weren't used in the films. I felt that if I had included any of these four protest poems in the actual narrative that is already rife and rich with poetry, this would have intrusively insinuated too many poems and too much local Motown material at points where it would have impeded the *forward global movement* of the dramatic dialogue between ornery old 'John-Paul' and 'The Eternal Presence.'

For Detroiters Resisting Emergency Management

So evil may no longer reign,
And lawless laws may not obtain,
Our Constitution must regain
Its constitutionality.
All reformative extremists
Must indeed become calamitous.
In Michigan, righteous extremity
Portends this all-cleansing calamity:
Then evil will *no longer reign,*
And lawless laws will *not obtain,*
And Constitutions will *regain*
Their constitutionality.

Where-O-Where?: A Motown Protest Song

(to be sung to the tune of 'Where-O-Where Has My Little Dog gone?')

Where-O-where has my little town gone?
O, where-O-where can it be?
With our assets sold for a sellout song,
O, where-O-where can it be?

Where-O-where has my old Motown *gone?*
O, where-O-where can it be?
With our schools cut short, and the banks cut long,
O where-O-where can it be?

Where-O-where has our fair justice *gone?*
O, where-O-where can it be?
With our laws cut short, and our judges wrong,
O where-O-where can it be?

Where-O-where have our nice homes *all gone?*
O, where-O-where will they be?
With our children locked out upon the lawn,
O, where-O-where will they be?

Where-O-where has our old safety *gone?*
O, where-O-where can it be?
With our cops cut short, and our pistols drawn,
O, where-O-where can it be?

Where-O-where has our old outrage *gone?*
O, where-O-where can it be?
With our lives cut short, and our guns all pawned,
O, where-O-where can it be?

Where-O-here have our free birthrights *gone?*
O, where-O-where can they be?
With our unions weak, and Jim Crow grown strong,
O, where-O-where can they be?

For Yusef

I wrote this poem for my young west-central Detroit friend Yusef Shakur, who grew up in my old Zone 8 neighborhood and spent nine years in prison for a crime he didn't do. I also wrote it for the untold thousands of our wrongly incarcerated young countrymen like Yusef who did prison time and have since been released to the streets, and who—due to draconian and unforgiving laws—are unable to find jobs that will pay a living wage so they can feed themselves and their families *legally.*

I still pray
There yet is time
For us not to have to hold
Our banks and judges hostage.

I still pray
There yet is time
To prevent a conflagration
In our subdivided nation
Because beautiful young black men
Are being murdered or unjustly jailed.

I still pray
There yet is time.

(Black lives matter.)

This next and fourth *localized* poem, which is in itself metaphorical, I had initially intended to include in order to illustrate the yawning societal chasm between two contiguous Southeastern Michigan counties (Wayne and Oakland), one nearly all-white and highly prosperous, the other heavily black and deeply impoverished—and the wealthier one having been governed for decades by an executive whose career in public life was launched in exclusionary, racialized controversy in the Oakland County town of Pontiac. I decided against including the poem because it would have required some interpretation and additional fictionalized narrative background for 'John-Paul Jones' that wouldn't necessarily have advanced the story:

Geography Juxtaposed:
The Count of Monte *Mephisto

(In abject *apologia* to Alexandre Dumas and his classic mid-nineteenth century novel *The Count of Monte Cristo*)

On my immutable moonscape of memory,
A county *I choose to call* 'Monte Mephisto'
Sits there due-northerly—cruelly contiguous
To my mystical 'earldom'-*in-metaphor home—*
While lying saber-split from that blue-collar 'earldom'
By a 'mountain' *that's actually* also *a* metaphor
Which ranges and rolls high and wide in between them.

He reigns by this border's dichotomous land
That nonetheless willingly deigns to remain

JUXTAPOSED.

*In reference to 'Mephistopheles,' another of several names for Satan—who by definition had to be a segregationist!

Appendix 'B'

As in Appendix 'A', in Appendix 'B' the author offers for the discerningly *activist* reader's edification some additional 'protest' poems—but some which this time are of a more *global* nature—*four poems* that might have been '*excessive baggage*,' had they, too, been pigeonholed into the *Poet-Emperor* narrative:

<u>Perpetuum Mobile*:*</u>
<u>*The Evolutionary*</u>
<u>Revolutionaries</u>

Revolution, evolution,
Evolution, revolution*;*
Erasing; chasing;
Running; racing;
Though unwilling,
Often killing;
Always thinking;
Usually linking;
Ever trucking;
Always bucking…

Revolution, evolution,
Revolution <u>sans</u> solution—
Conflict without <u>resolution</u>—
Fighting on and on *and* <u>ON</u>
Forever.

Comes the Revolution II

*Soaring lizards like *'the Donald'—*
Pterodactyls reincarnate—
Oftentimes will live to see their
Towers toppled. Thus we finally
Get to tear them

Down.

*Trump

Barreling Dogs of War:
The Canine *Crusade*

For lo these wild years in our crusade,
We have been akin to the lean wolf
That runs all night and every brutish day
To bring down cloven devils on the hoof.

Now we grizzled, panting/dashing dogs
Exhort you pups*:*
Our race is far from won—
To catch and kill the greedy corporate hogs,
Your *barreling is barely but* begun.

The CorpoRATocrats

Democracy*?? They tend* to ban *it*
All around our plundered planet—
Let's band *together to* demand *it*
Back *from bureaucrat and bandit!*

Appendix 'C'

And finally, your old poet-author presents this last appended poem which reflects his own overweening liberal philosophy, plus his hope for the successful mission of this egalitarian book and others with the same pro-democracy, anti-corporatocracy and anti-war mission and theme. Donizetti's 'Roberton Devereux Overture' with its recurring refrain 'America the Beautiful' is a reflective listening-piece for around the reading-time of this last little verse:

America, My Love

I've laughed and loved and lived in turn
With Arab, WASP, and Jew.
I've played with, grown with, taught, and learned
from Black, Malay, and Sioux.
I've reached in love to touch the face
Of someone short—and tall.
To run and win *the* human *race,*
We need to love us all.

Resources, References, Influences, & Inspirations

Ali, Muhammad, former world heavyweight boxing champion

Bloom, Allan, *The Closing of the American Mind,* Simon & Schuster, New York, 1987

Boggs, Grace Lee, Ph.D., 'Naming the enemy,' in her column *Living for Change*, the *Michigan Citizen*, February 8 – 5, 2014

Boyd, Melba Joyce, Ph.D., *Cat eyes and dead wood* (book of poetry), Fallen Angel Press, Highland Park, Michigan, 1978

Bradford, Reginald ('Reggie'), former Detroit Pershing High School, University of Michigan, and NCAA one-mile relay star

Braudel, Fernand, *A History of Civilizations*, translated by Richard Mayne, New York, the Penguin Press, 1994

Briscoe, Tom, boxing trainer and referee (deceased)

Brooks, Jr., the Rev. Arkles C., former Detroit Southeastern High School quarter-miler, three cited *jokes* told to the author

Bryson, Craig, piece on the author: 'Controversial leader forced district to question,' editorial in the *Rochester Clarion*, June 15, 1991

Camus, Albert, *The Plague; The Fall, Exile & the Kingdom; and Selected Essays,* New York: Every Man's Library, 1947

Carr, Henry, 1964 Olympian, Detroit Northwestern High School and Arizona State University (died in 2015)

Carr, Lloyd, former head football coach, the University of Michigan

Chambers, Jennifer, piece on the author: 'Ousted DPS chief sues EM, state,' the *Detroit News,* April 18, 2013

Chomsky, Noam, Ph.D., *The United States, Israel, and the Palestinians* (Updated Edition),Haymarket Books, 2014

Cunningham, Father Tom (deceased), director of Focus Hope, Detroit

Daggett, Willard R., paper: 'The Future of Vocational Education in the United States,' 1989

Doughty, Glenn, former Detroit Pershing High School, University of Michigan, and National Football League star with the old Baltimore Colts

Dyer, Wayne W., Ed.D., *Your Erroneous Zones,* Funk & Wagnalls, New York, 1969

Dzwonkowski, Ron, 'Author tells of fight for justice as teacher, activist' (review of the author's autobiographical *A Life on the RUN – Seeking & Safeguarding Social Justice*), the *Detroit Free Press,* April 18, 2010

Eggemeyer, Jean, 'Detroit's Fiery Schoolhouse Crusader,' (review of *A Life on the RUN*), *Dome Magazine*, January 16, 2010

Eliot, Thomas Stearns, quote from poem 'Burnt Norton,' in *T. S. Eliot and the Idealogy of Four Quartets,* by John Cooper, *Cambridge University Press, 2008*

Ellison, Ralph, *Invisible Man,* New York: Vintage Books, 1952

Fieger, Bernard, activist attorney (deceased)

Fieger, Geoffrey, activist attorney, Southfield, Michigan

Flam, Samuel, Ed.D., Superintendent (retired), Berkley (Michigan) Community Schools

Glatthorn, Allan, 'A Curriculum for the 21st Century,' *The Clearing House*, Vol. 62, #1, September, 1988

Goodwin, Doris Kearns, *Team of Rivals – The Political Genius of Abraham Lincoln*, Simon & Schuster, New York, 2005

Harris, Aurora, fragment of her poem 'Yurugu,' *Solitude of Five Black Moons,* Broadside Press/University of Detroit-Mercy Press, 2011

Hatcher, Clifford A., high school All-American quarter-miler, Detroit, Michigan (deceased)

Haywood, Spencer, former Detroit Pershing High School and National Basketball Association star

Hedges, Chris, Ph.D., *Death of the Liberal Class,* Nation Books, New York, 2010

Henig, Jeffrey R, Hula, Richard C., Orr, Marion, and Pedeseleaux, Deseree S., *The Color of School Reform - Race, Politics, and the Challenge of Urban Education*, Princeton University Press, Princeton, New Jersey, 1999

Hitchens, Christopher, *God Is Not Great,* Atlantic Books, 2007

The *Holy Bible (Old & New Testaments: King James* Version)

Holmes, David L., Wayne State University track coach between 1917 and 1958

Homer, *The Iliad,* translated by Robert Fitzgerald, Anchor Books: Garden City, New York, 1974

Horton, Willie (with Kevin Allen; foreword by Al Kaline), *The People's Champion,* Immortal Investments Publishing, Wayne, Michigan, 2005

Howell, Shea, Ph.D., 'Democracy shutoff,' in the column *Thinking for Ourselves* in the online *Living for Change News* published by the Boggs Center to Nurture Community Leadership, Detroit, Michigan, August 19, 2014

—, 'Fair water,' the *Michigan Citizen*, August 10 – 16, 2014

In Pursuit of a Dream Deferred, edited by Vina Kay, Gavin Kearney, and john a. powell, Peter Lang Publishing, Inc., New York, 2001

'Invisible Violence,' Editorial in the *Michigan Citizen,* August 17 – 23, 2014

I Said It and I Meant It (The Soul of DUPAAS [Detroit Unity Poets & Authors Society]*) Poetry Anthology,* 2012

Jackson, Murray, Ph.D., *Bobweaving Detroit – The Selected Poems of Murray Jackson,* African-American Life Series edited by Melba Joyce Boyd and Ron Brown, Wayne State University Press, 2004

Jenkins, Charley, 1956 Olympian, Villanova University

Keane, William G., Ph.D., Superintendent (retired), Oakland County Intermediate School District

Kennedy, Robert Fitzgerald (deceased)

Kick, Russ, *100 Things You're Not Supposed To Know*, Fine Communications, New York, 2003

King, Jr., the Rev. Dr. Martin Luther (deceased)

Kirschenbaum, Stuart, M.D., former boxing commissioner of the State of Michigan

Leon III, Ph.D., Wilmer J., 'ISIS and U.S. foreign policy: My enemy's enemy is not my friend,' *Trice Edney Newswire*, September 27, 2014

Lessenberry, Jack, 'The real meaning of the Great Flood,' *The Metro Times,* August 20 – 26, 2014

—, 'Why Wayne County matters' in *Politics and Prejudices, The Metro Times, July 9 – 15, 2014*

Liebler, M. L., Editor and Introducer, *Working Words – Punching the Clock and Kicking Out the Jams* (anthology), Coffee House Press, 2010

Lieblong, A. J., *The Earl of Louisiana,* Louisiana State University Press, 1986

Lipson, Dr. Greta B., Detroit-area author of children's books

Lobenthal, Richard, retired Director, Midwest Anti-Defamation League

Louis, Joe, (born Joseph Louis Barrow), former world heavyweight boxing champion from Detroit (deceased)

Lukacs, John, 'America's True Power,' *American Heritage* magazine, March, 1989

Maher, Bill, *New Rules*, Rodale Press, distributed by Holtzbrinck Publishers, 2005

McClellan, Keith, Ph.D., *The Hero Within Us – A History of Track & Field in the Twentieth Century from a Michigan Perspective,* Eastern Michigan Press, 2001

Melville, Herman, *Moby Dick*—quote from, on Page 66 of John G. Rodwan, Jr.'s philosophic book on boxing: *Fighters & Writers,* Mongrel Empire Press, Normal, Oklahoma, 2010

The *New York Times*, several articles

Orwell, George, *Nineteen Eighty-Four,* London: Secker &Warburg, *1949*

Obama, Barack H.

Owens, J. C. ('Jesse,') 1936 Olympian, the Ohio State University (deceased)

Owens, Keith, 'John Telford's dictionary for grownups, *What OLD MEN Know*, offers wisdom spiced with humor,' the *Michigan Chronicle*, March 23- 29, 2011

Pedroni, Thomas, Ph.D., Professor of Education, Wayne State University: extensive *research* regarding Detroit's K- 12 schools

Plato, *The Republic*, circa 347 (?) B.C.

Postman, Neil, and Weingartner, Charles, *Teaching as a Subversive Activity*, Delta Publishing, Inc., New York, 1969

Powell, john, and Telford, John, 'Race and Residential Segregation in Detroit,' in *America's Urban Crisis and the Advent of Color-Blind Politics – Education, Incarceration, Segregation, and the Future of U.S. Multi-Racial Democracy*—edited by Joshua A. Bassett and Curtis L. Ivery [Lanham; Boulder; New York; Toronto; & Plymouth, UK – Rowman & Littlefield Publishers, Inc., 2011]

—, 'Race problems stand in way of true growth,' the *Detroit Free Press*, May 5, 1999

Powell, john a., *Racing to Justice: Transforming our conceptions of Self and Other to Build an Inclusive Society*, Indiana University Press, 2012

'Prancing Poetry,' the *New Monitor*, August 14, 2014

Rhoden, George, 1952 Olympian, Morgan State College and Jamaica

Rice, John ('Jack'), track & football coach, Detroit Public Schools (deceased)

Rich, Wilbur C., *Coleman Young and Detroit Politics*, Wayne State University Press, Detroit, 1989

Robinson, 'Sugar' Ray (born Walker Smith, Jr. in Detroit in 1920), former world welterweight and middleweight boxing champion (deceased)

Robinson, Will, Detroit's path-breaking African-American high school coach and head basketball coach at Illinois State University, National Basketball Association team administrator, Detroit Pistons (deceased)

Rosenthal, A. M., 'U.S. ought to be fighting all religious persecution,' the *Detroit Free Press*, May 13, 1998

Ross, Alex, 'Onward and upward with the arts: *Deus ex Musica*,' the *New Yorker* magazine, October 20, 2014

Ross, Rev. Joan, Cathedral of the Blessed Sacrament, Detroit
Rowe, Rev. Edwin, retired pastor of Central United Methodist Church, Detroit
Russakoff, Dale, *The Prize - Who's in Charge of America's Schools?*, Houghton Mifflin Harcourt, Boston and New York, 2015
Sanders, Bernard, United States Senator from Vermont
Schmidt, Marilyn, 'How To Resolve Conflict,' *Wayne State* (periodical), fall, 1989
Schram, Hal, 'Inner city loses the good doctor,' story about the author in the sports section of the *Detroit Free Press, June 3, 1969*
Schultz, John M., Ph.D., Superintendent (retired), Rochester (Michigan) Community Schools
Scott, Louis, 1968 Olympian, Detroit's old Eastern High School and Arizona State University
Shakur, Yusef, *My Soul Looks Back,* Urban Guerilla Publishing, 2012
Southworth, Caleb, 'John Telford pours it on,' cover story in the May 22 - 28, 1991 *Metro Times* headlined 'John Telford: Rochester's maverick educator prepares for the next round'
Stephens, Thomas, Esq., several 2013/2014 online commentaries in the *Detroit Communicator*, a publication arm of D-REM (Detroiters Resisting Emergency Management)
Telford, Helen, 1907 – 1998, stellar kindergarten teacher
Telford, John (the elder), 1902 – 1987, boxer, coal-miner, and union steward
Telford, John, *A Comparison of student response to a collection of original stories, poetry, and discussion lessons,* doctoral dissertation, Wayne State University, 1968
—, 'Creative Insubordination,' the *Telford's Telescope Column* in the *Michigan FrontPage,* March 2, 2003
—, 'Didn't I warn you about Bush?', the *Telford's Telescope* in the *Michigan FrontPage, September 21, 2005*
—, 'DPS' sands are shifting like quicksand,' the *Michigan Citizen,* October 19th – 25th, 2014
—, 'Educate all our kids, not just the privileged,' the *John Telford* column in the *Observer/Eccentric* Newspapers, November 1, 1993

—, 'Engler ready to impose mandatory diet on many,' the *John Telford* column in the *Oakland Press,* March 9, 1997
—, 'Fascism & Classism in Detroit and Lansing,' DetroitCommunicator@gmail.com, December 21, 2013
—, 'Federated Regionalism can fulfill the dream,' the *Telford's Telescope Column* in the *Michigan Chronicle,* February 4-10, 2009
—, 'For students, *great* literature equals *relevant* literature' [italics inserted], the *Telford's Telescope Column* in the *Michigan FrontPage,* October 31, 2003
—, 'Ghettos, enclaves hinder equality,' the *Detroit Free Press,* October 12, 1987
—, 'Integrated schools pave way to open housing,' The *South End,* October 18, 1967
—, 'King's dream is still far from reality,' the *John Telford* column in the *Observer/Eccentric* Newspapers, January 20, 1994
—, 'Language and its implementation – key to it all,' the *John Telford* column in the *Observer/Eccentric* Newspapers, November 30, 1992
—, *the lifelong POETIC PRANCINGS of mad John,* DetroitINK Publishing, 2014
—, *A Life on the RUN – Seeking and Safeguarding Social Justice,* Harmonie Park Press, 2010 (see www.AlifeontheRUN.com)
—, *The Longest Dash,* published by *Track & Field News* Press, Los Altos, California, 1965 and 1971
—, 'Move to better schools: Madison District offers open enrollment, superior education,' the *Detroit Free Press,* April 16, 2009
—, 'Politically correct isn't always correct,' the *Telford's Telescope* column in the *Michigan FrontPage.* August 6, 2004
—, 'Prayers for our President,' the *Telford's Telescope* column in the *Michigan Chronicle,* February 10, 2010
—, 'Rebels, renegades, & revolution,' the *Telford's Telescope* column in the *Michigan Chronicle,* October 7, 2009
—, 'Rehabilitation and job training aid in transition,' the *Detroit Free* Press, January 25, 2002
—, 'Symptom of a sick society,' the *Telford's Telescope* column in the *Michigan Chronicle,* August 12 – 18, 2009

—, 'U.S. still a white supremacist nation,' The *Michigan Chronicle*, September 20- 26, 2006
—, 'We are all spiritually intertwined,' the *John Telford* column in the *Oakland Press,* September 26, 1991
—, *What OLD MEN Know—A Definitive Dictionary and Almanac of Advice,* Harmonie Park Press, 2010
—, 'What our next mayor must do,' the *Telford's Telescope Column* in the monthly *Detroit Native Sun*, June, 2014
—, 'A white man's case for affirmative action,' the *Telford's Telescope* column in the *Michigan FrontPage*, September 21, 2003
—, *Why You Didn't* Tell *Me That?? – A 'Foreign-Language' Approach to Teaching English,* a 1963 instructional booklet published by the Detroit Public Schools (this title features an 'Ebonic' expression—a subject-verb word-order reversal)
—, 'Why language matters,' the *Telford's Telescope* column in the *Michigan Chronicle*, April 2 – 8, 2008
—. 'Yesterday Is Tomorrow', poem by the author in *Prize Poets of 1966*, a publication of the Sharon (Connecticut) Creative Arts Foundation
Telford's Telescope [Third Annual]—*1990 Planning Paradigm* for *Discovering the Year 2000*, an administrative booklet published by the Rochester Community Schools' Division of Instruction
Tolan, Edward ('Eddie'), 1932 Olympian, Detroit Cass Technical High School and the University of Michigan (deceased)
Trimer, Margaret, 'School official leaves; his struggle goes on,' front-page story about the author in the *Detroit Free Press,* May 7, 1991
Voltaire (Francois Marie Arouet), *Candide,* Random House, Inc., 1928 (renewal copyright 1955 by illustrator Rockwell Kent and 1963 by Barron's Educational Series, Inc.)
Wilson, Ruben, 'Land of the free?', *Detroit Native Sun,* August, 2014
Wright, Lorenzo, 1948 Olympian, Detroit's old Miller High School and Wayne State University (deceased)
X, Malcolm, AKA 'Detroit Red,' born Malcolm Little (deceased)
Zaniewski, Ann, 'Educator and activist Telford joins Detroit mayoral race,' the Detroit *Free Press,* May 14, 2013
Zapata, Emiliano, Mexican revolutionary

Acknowledgements

I would like to express my gratitude to Prof. Joshua A. Bassett, Director of the Wayne County Community College District-Sponsored Institute for Social Progress, for taking time from his demanding schedule to write the lengthy and incisive Introduction to this book.

I also thank prominent Michigan poet and Wayne State University Professor M. L. ("Mike") Liebler for touting me as a 'well-known and talented poet' when I was still in fact better-known for my prose writings and my lifelong political hell-raising than for my verses—although (youthful *quarter-miling* aside) I have always regarded *versifying* to be what I do best.

In addition, I would like to acknowledge Dr. Wayne W. Dyer and Prof. john a. powell—my *protégés* and later my *compadres* of more than half-a-century—for their unflagging loyalty and friendship across the decades and the miles (and also the late Dr. Dyer for having particularly noted in his blurb for my book of poetry *Poetic Prancings* that I have a 'warrior's heart and a *poet's* soul'!).

I am unable to thank the semi-fictitious 'Balalaika Jones' for her patience with her semi-fictitious spouse 'John-Paul Jones the Third,' for indeed she had *little*. However, I *do* deeply thank her actual incarnate counterpart—my long-suffering *better half* Adrienne Telford (who really *did* fall and break her arm in July of 2014!)—for her praiseworthy patience during the daily and nightly hours within the two months when I shut myself away from her to write this existential exegesis and also engaged in my multiple other political activisms out in the field, often being obliged to leave her languishing behind on our lakeside patio, coffee in hand. One of the few times she *did* accompany me to hear me speak (this time at Cass Technical High School on March 9, 2015), she fell on black ice and broke her ankle in three places.

Lastly, although I do remain a reluctantly skeptical *agnostic* at best, I nonetheless thank the 'Great Eternal Presence' for (*actually*!) coming to me in a *deified* (??) dream and inspiring me to write this story featuring His/Its philosophical dialogues with 'John-Paul Jones the Third' regarding what the Empire of Earth—or *rather*, John-Paul's *preferred* *Democratic* Republic of the United States of America—should aspire again to *be*.

- John Telford
Poet, Author, confirmed Curmudgeon, and Doctor of Education,
Detroit, Michigan, July 4, 2016.

About your old activist agitator Author

Prize-winning poet/author/educator John Telford holds a bachelor's degree in the Liberal Arts and master's and doctoral degrees in Education from Michigan's Wayne State University in Detroit, where he has also taught—and where he was named the University's Distinguished Alumnus of the Year in 2001 for his social activism. He has been called a "human-rights legend' in southeastern Michigan. (More frequently—if somewhat less *kindly*—he has also been called a "lightning rod for controversy.") As a college administrator during the Vietnam War, he participated in protest marches on the Warren Tank Arsenal and was suspended for insubordination for bringing actress Jane Fonda and leaders of the Black Panthers to speak at the school.

Dr. Telford retired in 1991 from the deputy superintendency in the 98 percent white Rochester (Michigan) Community Schools, where affiliates of the Southeastern Michigan Skinheads shot bullets into his home at midnight for aggressively recruiting and hiring minority administrators and for establishing a holiday policy that was fair to non-Christian students. (The shooters were caught and went to prison.) After launching a multi-job professional comeback, Telford was subsequently fired from two non-consecutive executive directorships in the Detroit Public Schools for blowing the whistle on top officials whom he accused of being "inept and corrupt 'white supremacist fellow-travelers' in blackface." A frightened white school board fired him from the superintendency in another white suburb for recruiting and enrolling hundreds of Detroit students against the wishes of threateningly raucous white residents after those residents threatened to break their windows and egg their cars.

His intransigent social activism in the face of timid selection committees and nervous governing boards often cost him other superintendencies and professorships—an economically debilitating circumstance which once prodded him to versify, *We who put conscience above our careers / Are dying as a breed—and are deep in arrears.* Since his earliest days as an educator, he has recognized that in repressive regimes and other bedrock bureaucracies, it is almost solely the academicians on whose shoulders rests the weight of exposing the discrepancies between what those in power profess and what they too often actually practice. In the fall of 1989, he wrote in a publication of the school district where he was administering its division of instruction, "The fact that the institution we call 'school' is regarded as an 'agent of society' does not absolve it from the responsibility to serve as an agent for progressive reconstruction. The American public school may in a certain sense be an agent of our society, but it is far from being an agent of the *state*—and this is a fundamental difference. It is not American but Fascist political theory that would merge the will of society with the will of the government and would bestow power to the government to dictate what citizens should think and say. It is not the function of the educational leadership in any democratic community to be uncritical supporters of the status quo. If we do not fulfill our charge as educators to anticipate and then help to shape the future for the common good, we become mere tools of the state—prostitutes trading our ideas for a dubious security, a precarious status."

In that same publication, he also wrote:

"What I said in a *Detroit Free Press* article over two years ago [*and now 29 years* ago] has an even greater bearing today, to wit: 'We have allowed our great urban centers to become a kind of Casbah-style residential, economic, and educational Third World. In order to win in the global marketplace and in the morally murky waters of geopolitics, America must maximize and then capitalize on the talents of *every citizen*. This *cannot happen* in a racially segregated setting.'"

In accord with this professed commitment to integration and urban education, when On June, 14, 2012, a beleaguered Detroit Board of Education invited him—at his then-unlikely age of 76—to become the Superintendent of the city's embattled public schools, Dr. Telford accepted its invitation on the spot. When an emergency manager law that Michigan's citizens had voted to have repealed was reinstated the following year, the Detroit Public Schools' thus re-empowered Emergency Manager was enabled to fire him—and the EM promptly and enthusiastically *did so* on March 29, 2013, which was the day after the illegal law took effect. Federal litigation challenging the dubious constitutionality of that law is ongoing. On September 29, 2014, the Detroit school board availed itself of a clause in the law to vote to remove its emergency manager after a statutorily designated length of time (eighteen months) and brought the old educator/poet back to resume his duties as Superintendent. Litigation in this regard is also imminent at this writing.

An amateur boxing champion as a teen and an NCAA All-American and world-ranked quarter-miler as a WSU undergraduate senior in 1957, John Telford defeated the reigning Olympic 400-meter champion in time faster than his Olympic win and went undefeated at 400 meters touring Europe that summer as a member of the United States national team. He is in the University's Athletic Hall of Fame and the Detroit Public Schools' Sports Hall of Fame. A track in Detroit was named for him. In 1982, he received a Distinguished Educator Award from the Kettering Foundation-sponsored Institute for the Development of Educational Activities (IDEA).

Throughout the 1990s, Dr. Telford taught Education and Psychology courses at Oakland University in Rochester, Michigan and wrote regular columns for the *Oakland Press* and the *Observer/Eccentric* Newspapers, plus several periodic ones for the *Detroit Free Press*, the *Detroit News*, and other newspapers. Among his many additional pursuits, he has coached track champions at the high school and college levels. The Detroit Track & Field Old-Timers organization gave him its Lifetime Achievement Award in 2010, and the Detroit-based Joe Louis Memorial Foundation gave him its Spirit of the Champ Award in 2011 for his explosive autobiography *A Life on the RUN - Seeking and Safeguarding Social Justice*, which focused partially on the painful plight of the Detroit Public Schools and on the similar plights of America's other urban school districts. (As poet Telford once poeticized, *If you wish your life never to sit on the shelf, / You had better endeavor to write it yourself.*)

Dr. Telford is the author of more than a thousand newspaper columns and seven books (two as-yet unpublished). He now serves as the occasional Senior Advisor on Schools to Detroit Mayor Michael E. Duggan when he isn't playing his violin, boating, painting, penning poetry, or writing his monthly column in the *Detroit Native Sun*—an activist community newspaper, and writing periodic ones again in the *Michigan Chronicle*.

The John Telford Show airs every Sunday afternoon at 3:00 on Radio One NewsTalk1200 out of Detroit Station WCHB (simulcast on 99.9FM). He can be contacted at DrJohnTelfordEdD@aol.com and booked at (313) 460-8272 or at DrJohnTelford@gmail.com for presentations on

*Urban education,

*Poetry (recitals, workshops and book-readings regarding *poetic* [and also *prosaic*] composition),

*The strategic practice of 'Creative Insubordination' while asserting one's basic, God-given human rights,

*Motivating oneself and others,

*The art and science of training for and running the quarter-mile, and

*The art and science of remaining spiritually, cognitively, and emotionally *vibrant* while coping with life's many challenges, growing inevitably *older*, and endeavoring to stay 'above the grass' as long as healthfully possible.

His website is www.AlifeontheRUN.com.

Dr. Telford resides with wife *Balalaika*—er, that *is*, wife *Adrienne*—beside the Detroit River and in a getaway lakefront home north of Thirteen Mile Road in St, Clair Shores, Michigan. (The house just happens to be eerily similar to the one he depicts in this allegorical novelette, *The* Poet-*Emperor of EARTH—An In-Depth Dialogue with the Deity*, which also recounts some background incidents experienced by one of the book's two "immortal" protagonists that were also experienced by its very *mortal* author.) In April 2016, he joined with the Detroit Public School Board and some DPS parents and students to sue the Governor of Michigan and DPS "emergency" managers appointed by the Governor.

He is confident that this lawsuit on behalf of the children will ultimately be successful.

Books by Dr. John Telford

The lifelong POETIC PRANCINGS of mad John—with an Introduction by Prof. Rhoda Stamell (author of *Detroit Stories* and *The Art of Ruin*) : DetroitINK Publishing, 2014

Creative INSUBORDINATION – 40 Successful Strategies—with an Introduction by retired Detroit Public Schools and Taylor, Michigan Schools principal Adrienne Lee Telford, M.A.: Harmonie Park Press, 2013

What OLD MEN Know – A Definitive Dictionary and Almanac of Advice—with an Introduction by Dr. Wayne W. Dyer (author of *Your Erroneous Zones, Pulling Your Own Strings, The Sky's the Limit,* and *Gifts from Eykis*) : Harmonie Park Press, 2010

A Life on the RUN – Seeking and Safeguarding Social Justice: Harmonie Park Press, 2010 (This is the author's autobiography, with an Introduction by Prof. john a. powell, the author's former student, who now is the Executive Director of the University of California at Berkeley-based Haas Institute for a Fair and Inclusive Society

The LONGEST DASH – a 'Running Commentary' on the Quarter-Mile : Track & Field News Press, 1965 and 1971 (out of print)

Will the FIRST – The Saga of Sports/Civil-Rights Pioneer Will Robinson—with an Introduction by former old Detroit Miller

High School and WSU All-American cager, Harlem Globetrotter, and Detroit Public Schools principal Charles (Charlie 'King Snake') Primas. (Robinson was the first African-American head basketball coach in NCAA Division One and the first black executive in the National Basketball Association [NBA], among many other *firsts*), DetroitINK Publishing, 2015

Book Manuscripts by the Author That Are As-Yet-Unpublished

The Eye in the Emerald (a novel set in fifteenth-century Scotland and dedicated to 'little Katherine' [Katherine Faye Helen Telford Garrett, the author's then-five-year-old and now 42-year-old daughter])

My Name Is DETROIT! - *Manifold* Motown *Memories in* Verse

Paeans of praise for The Poet-Emperor of EARTH and its author

"Dr. Telford is the champion of the underdog." - Dennis Archer, former Mayor of Detroit

"Were I simply to call this luminous little book '*unique*,' it wouldn't do justice to its sheer splendor. *The* Poet-*Emperor* is the most enlightening *parabolic parody* that I have ever read. A magnificent *hybrid* of *morality tale*/fabulous work of *fiction*, its timelessly righteous message packs a potent punch, as one would naturally expect from its one-time-boxer author." – **Tom Bleakley**, **Esq**., author and nationally prominent trial lawyer, former (1958) Detroit Public High School League Champion, one-mile run, St. Clair Shores, Michigan

"'The *Poet*-Emperor of EARTH' is a lofty yet fitting title for a liberal-philosophic novel that again brings us the sometimes hilarious but also often heart-wrenching and frighteningly prophetic higher-order insights of the activist author/poet Telford. As in his earlier works, his right-on-target rhetorical reflections offer the discerning reader a profoundly thought-provoking analysis of the proverbial 'who, what, when, where, why, and how' of egalitarian activism. Much of what you didn't know about the imperiled state of our city, state, nation, and *planet* you *will* know after you have internalized the message of this *must-read* book and digested its ten life-preserving proposals to the U.S. Congress." – **Greg Dunmore**, Pulsebeat Arts, Entertainment, and Culture journalist, Television Channel 20, Detroit

"John Telford has a *warrior's* heart and a *poet's* soul." – **Dr. Wayne Dyer**, world-renowned author and lecturer, late of Maui, Hawaii

"If you're a) *stupid*, and/or b) *close-minded* (*e.g.*, an inveterate and incontrovertible *Republican* with a consistent annual income of less than $300,000), don't even *attempt* to comprehend the mind-expanding message of this urgent exegesis." – **Alte R. Ego*rra*, Ph.D.**, Detroit educator

"John Telford's strength, integrity, and unfailing commitment to humanitarian causes actually *would* make him a great celestial choice to rule a hypothetical 'Empire of Earth.' Both his poetry and his prose are absolutely *mesmerizing*, and his sprinkles of humor—coupled with a talent for telling a story with an intensely *personalized* message—eloquently incorporate the Judeo-Christian values that all humankind desperately needs to embrace at this crucial time in human history. I congratulate him on yet another enlightening and rewarding 'read'!" – **Dr. Gary A. Faber**, Superintendent (retired), West Bloomfield (Michigan) Schools

"Set in the Earth-year of 2014 as our warring planet wallows deep within its perpetual orgy of killing, this fascinating, fast-moving dialogue between God and man is both grippingly captivating and profoundly thought-provoking. 'Superman', 'Batman', 'Spiderman', and 'Captain Marvel' have presumably all had their fruitless chance to save us Earthlings from ourselves—and Buddha, Mohammed, and even *Jesus* have taken earlier cracks at it as well. Planet Earth nonetheless continues to languish in its murderous morass of injustice and greed. Finally, an exasperated Deity (the 'Great Eternal Presence')—Who/Which has become disillusioned with democracy's evident ineffectiveness in maintaining worldwide peace with justice—deputizes poet/philosopher/diehard Democrat 'John-Paul Jones the Third' to fix things *undemocratically* and in fact *imperially.*

"Protagonist 'Jones' also just happens to bear a remarkable (and deliberate) similarity to the book's prolific author/poet Telford. Read on to see whether the world is saved through this authoritarian method and via this sometimes contentious dialogue between The *Democracy-Doubting* Deity and a *Prophetically Poeticizing* old Democrat—but no peeking before you get to the end!" - **Michael 'Doc' Holbrook,** Social/Political Activist, *Fen Shui* Imaging Consultant, and Board Member of the Boggs Center, Detroit

"An *ideologue*, it's certain I'm not—
I'm not even a true Democrat.
Still I enjoyed how *playfully* (or *not*?)
This book pins Republicans onto the mat.
Its *real* recollections make its fast-moving story
A lot more believable than mere allegory.
I envision the words rolling right off his fingers
As Telford typed this most intriguing satire—
And *insightful symbolism* lingers,
Because the situation is most definitely dire.
While I can't always concur, I remain wonder-ING
What the world would be like with this Emperor/KING!" – **Stephen Korotkin**, M.D., the author's cardiologist (and an aspiring sometime poet), Bingham Farms, Michigan

"*The* Poet-*Emperor of EARTH* is a fascinatingly fantastic yet philosophic approach to the hoped-for prospect of an alternative (and fairer) future—not only for Detroit and Michigan, but for America and all of the planet. This unique allegorical novel is spellbindingly provocative reading for the genuinely open-minded. It is also a bright revelation for those readers whose minds aren't quite closed yet and thus can perhaps be prodded and galvanized into righteously democratic activism." - **Tom Nelson**, former police sergeant, retired Great Lakes CEO, columnist, MENSA member, and former Detroit public school teacher (and the author's graduate student at Oakland [Michigan] University)

"Telford possesses an incredible ability to tell a captivating tale with poignancy, humor, and depth. As in much of his previously published poetry, mystical overtones resonate in this spellbinding allegorical novella." – **Keith Owens**, author, columnist, and senior editor, the *Michigan Chronicle*

"John Telford is a rebel, a renegade, and a Renaissance man." – **Huel Perkins**, Fox TV2News anchor, Detroit

"John Telford was my teacher at Detroit Southeastern High School in the early 1960s. As a consummate and fearless advocate for human rights and as the recent Superintendent of Detroit Public Schools in tumultuous times, everything that Dr. Telford has written about in his books, his poetry, and his newspaper columns he has also lived through and *lived by* during his long and productive life. These visceral experiences reverberate resoundingly in many parts of this book." – **Prof. john a. powell**, Executive Director of the Haas Institute, the University of California at Berkeley—and a former national legal director of the ACLU

"Dr. Telford deftly weaves a hypnotically hallucinatory world that supplants the equally surreal one we live in. Here is a sardonically socio-philosophical allegory that cuts far down into our consciousness and *consciences* to make us reflect *really deeply*—while also often managing to make us *laugh* as well." – **Tom Stephens, Esq.,** activist Attorney and Board member of D-REM (Detroiters Resisting Emergency Management), Detroit, Michigan

"Once again, Dr. John Telford has delved into his depthless reservoir of raw experience to confront the reader with yet another sparkling torrent of words that sweeps us this time to an idealistically fantastic plane, enveloping our souls in a captivating current that magnetizes hearts and minds. In *The* Poet-*Emperor of EARTH,* haunting passages of dark humor and sheer, unadulterated genius are to be found. As I was upon first encountering former world-class sprinter Telford's autobiographical *A Life on the RUN,* I again find myself in willing thrall to this iconic writer who may one day be proclaimed the foremost force in the activist world of liberal literature. Join me to bask in the bright effluence of an earthily *earthly* yet profoundly *spiritual* book that is far more than mere words on paper. This laser-like allegorical dialogue between God and man *lives* and *breathes* with a rare brilliance that comes to us without reservation or apology." – **Greg Thrasher**, Radio/Television Commentator, Washington, D.C.

Index & Cast of Characters—Fictional and Otherwise

A

Adam (biblical figure) 24
Adolf der Adder (poem) 56
Air Force One 113
Albom, Mitch 126
Alexander the Great of Macedon 33, 114
Alexander VI, the Borgian Pope 35, 36
Al-Qaeda 69
Amin, Idi 34
Andersen, Hans Christian 115
Ane'e, Natasha 127
Animal Farm (Orwell) 92
Annie Speaks (Cullen) 126
Anti-Defamation League 76
Aristotle 29, 30, 40, 66
Armenian massacre, 1915 35
Art of Ruin, The (Stamell) 126
Atilla the Hun 33
Atlantis 126

B

'Balalaika Jones' 9, 167
Baraka, Amiri. *See* Jones, Leroi
Barclay, Geraldine (National Organization for Women official) 76
Barry, Marion 73
Bassett, Joshua A. 75, 167
Batista, Fulgencio 34
'Badderson,' L. Brooks 107
Battle Hymn of the Republic 99
'Bear' (nebula) 32
Beethoven 66, 67
Beginning of Worlds 129
Bellant, Russ 126
Ben Gurion, David 41
'Big Bang' Theory 85
Black Liberation Front 76
black-on-black violence 123
Black Panthers 76, 169
Blaney, George 108
Bloom, Allan 66
Boehner, John 114

Boggs, Grace Lee 5, 73, 75
Boggs, Jimmy 73
Bonaparte, Napoleon (emperor) 34
Borgia, Cesare 35
Boyd, Melba Joyce 127
Buddha, the 43, 179
Burns, Robert 17
'Burnt Norton' (poem) 133
Bush, George W. 35, 70, 121, 122

C

Cain (biblical figure) 28
Caligula (Roman emperor) 33
Carr, Henry (Olympian) 108
Carter, Jimmy 43
Cawley, Rex (Olympian) 108
Cezanne, Paul 125
Charles I (King of England) 34
Cheney, Richard 55, 70, 104
Churchill, Winston 42
Clinton, Hillary R. 43
Confucius 43, 66
Count of Monte Cristo, The (Dumas) 154
'Crab' (nebula) 32
Cromwell, Oliver 34
Crow, Jim 73
Cullen, Collette, author of Play *Annie Speaks* 126
Cunningham, Fr. Tom 66

D

Dali, Salvadore 125
De Gaulle, Charles 42
Detroit Stories (Stamell) 126
Detroit Unity Poets and Authors Society (DUPAAS) 161
Diaz, Porfirio 34
Dickenson, Emily 17
Diogenes 49
Doc. *See* Holbrook, Michael
Doherty, J. K. (Olympian) 108
Dr. Phil 66
'Dublin', Michael A. 101, 102
Dumas, Alexandre 66
DUPAAS. *See* Detroit Unity Poets and Authors Society
Duvalier, Francois 34
Dyer, Wayne W. 66, 75, 167, 178

E

Ebola virus 132
Eden (biblical garden) 95
Ego*rra*, Alte R. (imaginary commentator) 178
Einstein, Albert 49, 84, 85, 86
Eliot, T. S. 17, 133
Elizabeth I (Queen of England) 41
Elysian Fields 95
EU. *See* European Union
Euclid 86
European Union 90

F

Faber, Gary A. 178
Farley, Reynolds 5
Farouk (King of Egypt) 34
Federated Regionalism 49, 50
feminism 98
Fifty Cent 66
Fonda, Jane 169
Forché, Carolyn 18
Fox News 82
Frederickson, Donald 126
Freud, Sigmund 66
Frost, Robert 18, 66

G

Gates, Henry Louis 5
General Motors 71, 108
Genghis Khan 33
George III (King of England) 20, 34
Ghandi, Mohandas 41, 73, 145
Giovanni, Nikki 18
Goldberg, Whoopie 43

Gore, Al 72
governmental tax break 147
Governor Sniper. *See* Rip Sniper
Gray Panthers 76
Great Eternal Presence, The 17, 19, 21, 23, 24, 26, 32, 55, 68, 87, 99, 101, 113, 119, 138, 151
Guevera, Che 42
Guyette, Curt 126

H

Hall, Darnell (Olympian) 108
Hamas 69
Hammarskjold, Dag 41
Harris, Alford G. 127
Harris, Aurora 17, 127
Henderson, Stephen 126
Henry VIII (King of England) 34
Hitler, Adolf 56
Holbrook, Michael 179
Homer (poet) 17
Horace (poet) 17
Housman, A. E. (poet) 17
Howell, Sharon 126
Hubbard, William DeHart (Olympian) 108
Hughes, Langston (poet) 17
Huguenots 34

I

Inquisition, the 34
Institute for Social Progress 5, 75
Isis 23, 69, 121

J

Jackson, Andrew 35
Jagger, Mick 66
Jefferson, Thomas 42
Jesus Christ 42, 43
John Paul Jones (American naval captain) 20
Johnson, Lyndon 35
Jones, Hayes (Olympian) 108
'Jones, John-Paul III' (fictitious protagonist) 4, 7, 8, 11, 12, 13, 15, 17, 19, 20, 23, 24, 25, 29, 31, 32, 33, 34, 37, 39, 40, 42, 43, 45, 46, 47, 50, 53, 55, 57, 60, 61, 63, 64, 65, 66, 67, 70, 74, 75, 76, 77, 79, 80, 83, 84, 85, 86, 87, 88, 89, 91, 96, 97, 98, 100, 101, 102, 103, 106, 107, 109, 112, 113, 117
Jones, Leroi 17

K

Keller, Helen 126
Kennedy, Robert F. 41
Khmer Rouge 121
Kilpatrick, Kwame 73
Kim Jong Un 110
King, Martin Luther, Jr. 8, 41, 66, 146
kings. *See* names of individual kings
Klingons 83
Kozma, Thomas William 126
Krysan, Maria 5

L

Landry, Robert 126
Lao-Tze 43
La Raza 76
Lautrec, Henri de Toulouse- 125
Lazarus (biblical figure) 42
Lemmons, Lamar, III 108
Lenin, Vladimir 42
Lessenberry, Jack 126
Liebler, M. L. 17, 167
Lincoln, Abe 42
Lincoln, Abraham. *See* Lincoln, Abe
Lincoln Memorial (Washington DC) 105
Lindsay, Vachel 17

Lizst, Franz 66
Longfellow, Henry Wadsworth 17
Lorca, Federico Garcia 17
Louis XIV (King of France) 34
L'Ouverture, Toussaint 42

M

Machiavelli, Niccolò 145
Maher, Bill 43
Malcolm X 42
Mandela, Nelson 41, 42
Mann, Thomas 66
Mao Tze-Tung 34
Marable, Manning 5, 73, 75
Marie Antoinette (queen) 51
Marshall, Thurgood 41
Marx, Groucho 42
Marx, Karl 42, 91
Massey, Douglass 5
Matisse, Henri 125
McGraw, Philip. *See* Dr. Phil
Meir, Golda 41
Mendel, Gregor 86
Mephistopheles (Satan) 154
Metalious, Grace 66
Michelangelo (Michaelangelo di Lodovico Bounarroti Simoni) 24
Milton, John (poet) 17
Mobutu, Sei Seke 34
Mohammed 43, 179
Montgomery, Wardell (poet) 127
Moral of the Sagacious Old Man on a Mountaintop 130
More, Sir Thomas 91
Moses (biblical figure) 41
Mother Teresa 41
Murdoch, Rupert 82
'Murphy' 86
Mussolini, Benito 34

N

NAACP 76
National Organization for Women 76
nebulas
'Bear' 32
'Crab' 32
neo-Jim Crowism 48
Nero (Roman emperor) 33
Netanyahu, Benjamin 43
Newton, Isaac 86
New World Order 40, 62, 100, 105, 113, 114, 125
Nicholas II (Russia's czar) 34
Niebuhr, Reinhold 41, 66
Nietzsche, Friedrich 66
Nixon, Richard 55, 66
NOW. *See* National Organization for Women

O

Obama, Barack 43, 44, 46, 47, 101, 106, 114, 115
Olympians. *See* individual names of Olympians

P

Pahlavi, Reza 34
Pandora's Box 93
Papa Doc. *See* Duvalier, Francois
Pascal, Blaise 86
People for the Ethical Treatment of Animals. *See* PETA
Perkinson, Jim (poet) 127
Perlman, Itzak 66
Peron, Juan 34
PETA 120
Pharaohs, the 33
Philip II (Spanish king) 34
Pilate, Pontius 59
Pius XII (pope) 26, 36
Plato 29, 30, 49, 66, 91, 145
Plautus 126

Plumpe, Robert 102, 108
poems 12, 15, 16, 17, 30, 52, 56, 57, 58, 121, 122, 124, 127, 133, 141, 142, 149, 151, 152, 153, 154, 155, 156, 157
poets. *See* names of individual poets
Pol Pot (Cambodian dictator) 34
Pound, Ezra (poet) 18
Powell, john a. 167
Putin, Vladimir 34

R

racial integration 148
Randall, Dudley (poet) 17
RDTDES. *See* Resource-Driven and Technology-Driven Economic System
Reagan, Ronald 41
Reconstruction 74
Resource-Driven and Technology-Driven Economic System (RDTDES) 91, 112, 125
Richelieu, Jean du Plessis de (cardinal and persecutor or the Huguenots) 34
'Rip Sniper' 107, 114
Rivers, Joan 43
'Robber,' Roy 108, 109, 111
Rodin, Auguste 125
Roosevelt, Eleanor 41
Rousseau, Jean-Jacques 66
Rowe, Rev. Edwin 66
Rustin, Bayard 73

S

Sadat, Anwar 41
Sartre, Jean-Paul 49
Schatmeyer, Matthew (poet) 127
Schauer, Mark 11, 102, 114
Shabazz, Khadijah (poet) 127
Shakespeare, William (poet) 17
Shakoor, Satori (poet) 127
Shakur, Yusef (poet) 126
Sharpe, Sherina (poet) 127
Sherman, Angelo 126
Simon Peter the Fisherman 41
Sistine Chapel 24
Sitting Bull 37
Socrates 27, 29, 40, 41
Southern Christian Leadership Conference 76
Spinoza, Benedictus de 49
SS (Schutzstaffel) 56
Stachurski, Anthony (poet) 127
Stalin, Josef 34
Stamell, Rhoda 175
  Art of Ruin, The 126
  Detroit Stories 126
Stanton, Tom 126
St. Clair Shores 11
Stephens, Thomas 126, 181
Sugrue, Thomas 5
Sullivan, Annie 126

T

Team for Justice 179
Telford, Frank 43
Telford, Helen 42
Telford, Jeff 87
Telford, John 65, 168, 175, 178, 181
Third World, the 116
Thomas, Clarence 55, 73
Thomas, Dylan (poet) 17
Tolan, Eddie (Olympian) 108
Tonton Macoute 121
Trump, Donald 114, 115
Trump Tower 111, 114
Tutu, Archbishop Desmond 43

U

United Nations General Assembly 117
United Nations, the 71
Urban League 76
Utopia 91

V

Vatican, the 26, 27
Verizon 82
Virgil (poet) 17
Vlad (the Transylvanian Impaler) 34
Vodafone 82
Voltaire (Francois Marie Arouet) 66

W

Warhol, Andy 67
Washington, George 42
WCHB NewsTalk1200 (Detroit) 11
West, Cornel 5
Whitman, Walt (poet) 17
Wilhelm II (Germany's Kaiser) 34
Williams, Lauryn (Olympian) 108
Williams, Mildred (poet) 127
Williams, Robin 43
'Winged Victory of Samothrace' 126
WNUC LP/FM 96.7 Detroit 148
Wordsworth, William (poet) 17, 142
Wright, Lorenzo (Olympian) 108

X

Xerxes 33

Y

Yeats, W. B. (poet) 17

Z

Zapata, Emiliano 42

CPSIA information can be obtained
at www.ICGtesting.com
Printed in the USA
FFOW04n0448191116
29485FF

9 781682 893005